Beryl Bainbridge is one of the greatest living English novelists. She is the author of seventeen novels, two travel books and five plays for stage and television. Her novels, *Master Georgie*, *Every Man for Himself* and *According to Queeney* were shortlisted for the Booker Prize, and *Every Man for Himself* was awarded the Whitbread Novel of the Year Prize. She won the Guardian Fiction Prize with *The Dressmaker* and the Whitbread Prize with *Injury Time*. *The Bottle Factory Outing*, *Sweet William* and *The Dressmaker* have been adapted for film, as has, most recently, *An Awfully Big Adventure*, which starred Hugh Grant and Alan Rickman. Beryl Bainbridge was born in Liverpool and now lives in north London.

Also by Beryl Bainbridge

FICTION

According to Queeney
An Awfully Big Adventure
Another Part of the Wood
The Birthday Boys
The Bottle Factory Outing
Collected Stories
The Dressmaker
Every Man for Himself
Filthy Lucre
Harriet Said
Injury Time
Master Georgie
Mum and Mr Armitage
Northern Stories (ed. with David Pownall)
A Quiet Life
Sweet William
Watson's Apology
A Weekend with Claude
Winter Garden

NON-FICTION

English Journey, or the Road to Milton Keynes
Forever England: North and South
Something Happened Yesterday

YOUNG ADOLF

BERYL BAINBRIDGE

An *Abacus* Book

First published in Great Britain by
Gerald Duckworth & Co. Ltd in 1978
This edition published by Abacus in 2003

A CIP catalogue record for this book is available from
the British Library.

ISBN 0 349 11613 X

Typeset in Baskerville MT by
Palimpsest Book Production Limited, Polmont, Stirlingshire

Printed and bound in Great Britain by Clays Ltd, St Ives plc

Abacus
An imprint of
Time Warner Books UK
Brettenham House
Lancaster Place
London WC2E 7EN

www.TimeWarnerBooks.co.uk

FOR LUVELY DON MACKINLAY

1

There had been a nasty incident, half-way between France and England, when young Adolf, turning in a moment of weakness to take a last look at the hills of Boulogne, had come face to face with a man wearing a beard and thick spectacles. For several seconds the two strangers had stood on the wind-swept deck and stared at one another. I shall control myself, thought Adolf. I will not run. Accordingly he had strolled in a leisurely fashion away from the stranger until, arriving at a convenient flight of stairs, he had bolted below deck and locked himself in the gentlemen's lavatory.

There for some time he had studied his passport and his papers, made out in the name of Edwin, his dead brother, and wondered miserably if it was likely that the Austrian military authorities would detail an official to shadow him across Europe. It was odd they had known he would be on this particular steamer. Was it possible that his half-sister Angela had reported him to the police? She had been in a morbid frame of mind when he visited her in Linz; her conversation had centred mainly on the last painful moments of her husband, the tax inspector, and the present state of his grave: some sort of animal was disturbing the top soil. Her finger-nails, Adolf noticed, had constantly raked the smooth surface of the tablecloth. She had smiled once in four hours – when reading aloud part of the seven-page letter recently arrived from England. Misunderstanding that smile, he had been foolish enough to laugh openly at the mention of safety razors. It was then that Angela had rounded on him, implying that he too lacked business ability and was in no position to criticise anybody. He had left abruptly, but not before pocketing the money she had placed ready for him on the dresser. It was true that on several previous occasions he had been forced to accept small sums from her, but in a sense he was merely borrowing money that had belonged to him in the first place. Perhaps it was not his sister but the lamplighter, Josef Greiner, who had betrayed him – that so-called friend who only two days ago had cut his hair for noth-ing. Had there not been something sinister in the way Greiner – a man often to be found rolling in the gutter – had fastidiously spread newspaper on the linoleum floor of the Männerheim lounge?

At last, maddened by doubt and repeated blows on the

panelling of the door, Adolf had flung back the catch and run savagely up the companionway to confront his pursuer. He would not hide like a fox in a hole. He had run with such swiftness that the wind had caught his cap and lifted it from his head. But though he had circled the deck for an hour or more he had been unable to find the bearded man. Nor, when he had retraced his steps and gone below in search of it, could he find his blown-away cap. Man and hat had disappeared in mid-channel.

Now young Adolf was sitting in the corner of a railway compartment, engrossed in a book. He had been reading for six hours, sometimes the same page, over and over. He read because by this time he was faint from lack of food, and because it seemed to him in his famished state that whenever he carelessly allowed himself to glance upwards from the page the numerous occupants of the carriage were eating. Their faces turned instantly to his; they made those small gestures – a slight lifting of the shoulders, a clearing of the throat – preparatory to offering him something. Even when he was careful only to look out of the window, he imagined he saw mouths reflected in the glass, steadily munching, imitating those other bedraggled beasts that cropped the grass beside the railway line. So he kept his head down as the train travelled slowly northwards beneath rain-filled skies and read and re-read the story of Old Shatterhand, chief of the white settlers of Texas and Arizona pledged to annihilate the fiendish Ogellalah Indians.

Through a landscape shimmering with heat Old Shatterhand rode like the devil himself into the encampment. Sunlight glinting off the barrel of his gun, he routed the cowardly redksins and took prisoner the warrior Nantaquond. Even now, Nantaquond lay staked out in the dust, naked as a babe; above him straddled Shatterhand holding aloft a leather pouch, from which dripped a thin trickle of wild honey that laced in golden strands the bloodstained limbs of the captive warrior – there, where his limp manhood lolled, mauve against his thigh. In the heavens of the Wild West, specks of dirt on the blue cloth of the sky, flies gathered in a quivering arrow and hummed downwards to the fallen Nantaquond. 'I am great,' hollered Old Shatterhand. 'I am glorious.'

Only at these triumphant and concluding words did Adolf put down his book. Immediately he was aware of the rumblings of his stomach. He dug his fists into his empty belly and affecting an interest in the view pressed his cheek to the window pane and squinted along the track. The train, buffeted by wind, was swaying over the steel lattice of a bridge, high above the silted estuary of a river. In the distance some kind of tower, complete with battlements, rose into the sky. From the outer wall a balcony hung, supported by winged angels carved in stone, on which a uniformed official stood as though behind a waterfall, holding a flag. Torrents of rain, spilling from the ramparts above, fell on to the red gravel of the track and sprayed the carriages ahead. Afterwards Adolf was inclined to think of his whole journey as one long approach to this dark fortress on the horizon; in reality he had no sooner caught sight of the building than it was upon him. The man in uniform, standing there like an heroic character in some opera, served no visible purpose. He had neither machinery to work, nor signal to operate; the flag he so uselessly held clung like a rag to the lapels of his braided jacket. The carriage rocked as it drew level with the tower – Adolf peered directly up at the balcony. He saw an angel, whose stone cheeks dripped with rain, and the face of the man, looking down. For an instant their eyes met. The man's mouth, set in a wild beard pulled by the wind, began to open. Then a long plume of smoke, spurting from the squat funnel of the engine ahead, floated backwards and whirled about the tower. The train passed by.

It was almost three o'clock in the afternoon. The passengers started to prepare themselves for arrival; they shook the crumbs from their clothes and kept an anxious eye on the weather. It was too soon to lift down the luggage from the rack. Adolf remained hunched in his seat, one hand shielding his face. He had the absurd idea that overhead the bearded man crouched waiting on the roof of the train, and yet he couldn't help but yawn repeatedly. It was as though he was a schoolboy again, making the journey from his home in Leonding, through just such a landscape of pale fields edged with mud, to the Realschule in Linz. Ahead of him stretched a day of unutterable boredom. In the gloomy building on the Steinstrasse he would attempt to memorise certain principles of mathematics or paragraphs of French and, failing, slump feebly over his books, listening to the squeak of chalk on the blackboard, until his eyelids closed and he felt he existed in some void between life and death, mindless, like an animal hibernating in the dark. It would be better if he never reached his destination. Spaced out across the hills stood the crumbling watch-towers, monuments to a time when Austria feared invasion by the armies of Napoleon. The rain flattened the grass that grew among the ruins and blew inwards over the flooded meadows to beat against the windows of the train. He had only to lift his head to see how the entire world wept.

While he was sleeping, the train plunged into the hills surrounding the city and entered a massive tunnel blasted from yellow sandstone. His fellow passengers hauled down their baggage and dragging open the compartment door stumbled into the corridor. Someone trod on Adolf's foot. He woke to darkness and confusion. The carriage was swaying so violently that he was forced to cling with both hands to the edge of his seat. Outside the window, a wall of rock, lit at intervals by flickering jets of gas, towered above him. Just when he thought he must be dashed to the floor, the train rumbled out of the tunnel and slid beneath a vaulted roof of iron and glass into Lime Street Station.

Hatless, his only luggage a book on Shatterhand of the Wild West, young Adolf had arrived in Liverpool.

2

Crossing Upper Parliament Street in a downpour of rain, Alois swung up his stick and hailed a taxi-cab.

'We shouldn't have,' said Bridget, thankfully climbing into the vehicle.

'It's a sensible extravagance,' her husband explained. 'Your boots are letting in the water.' His own footwear was in splendid condition, as was his overcoat and homburg hat – but then a man embarking on a new business venture couldn't go about looking like a derelict. In the fist of his pigskin glove he held a bunch of purple violets.

'In the long run,' said Bridget, 'it might be more sensible if I had a new pair of boots.' But she wasn't criticising him in any serious way. Whatever his faults, meanness wasn't one of them. After three years of marriage he sat with his arm around her waist, and it pleased her, though she knew there was nothing exclusive in this show of affection: he regularly embraced Mr Meyer and Dr Kephalus; sometimes he stroked the shoulder of Mary O'Leary, and she was no sight to break the bank: he liked touching people – it was due to him being a foreigner.

Bridget had first met him in the saddling enclosure at the Dublin horse show. Introducing himself as Alois Hitler from Austria, he had bowed over her hand; his little finger, encircled by a ruby ring, had grazed her wrist. She had fallen in love instantly, as though struck down by influenza. He wore a cream-coloured waistcoat with a heavy silver chain slung from pocket to pocket; hooked over his arm he carried an ivory walking stick tipped with a handle of gold. She had stood transfixed, the horses tossing their heads and side-stepping, her own head on a level with his chest. Stabbed in his tie was a glittering pin embellished with a single pearl. He was dazzling in the sunlight.

Now, as he leant across her to gaze out of the window, Alois's moustaches brushed her cheek. She knew it was probably a woman who was attracting his attention, but she didn't fret. There was no harm in his looking. Not today. It wasn't the moment for him to leap out of the cab and out of her life. Last night, after hearing she had spent three hours preparing food for the arrival of their guest, he had gone so far as to call her the best wife in the world. She would have preferred to cook some sort of Austrian dish, but Mr Meyer had been against it. 'My dear child,' he had protested, 'would you care to go all that way over land and sea to be served a plate of cabbage and boiled beef . . . with the prunes and custard to follow?' As he was offering her the use of the kitchen range in the basement, Bridget felt obliged to accept his culinary advice. She did however manage to avoid descending to the basement at the time Mr Meyer suggested. She said she must visit the wash-house during the morning; it would be more convenient to wait until after tea when the baby had been put to bed. Fortunately Mr Meyer left the house every morning at six o'clock to play his violin in the supper rooms of the Adelphi Hotel.

'I wish I hadn't done mutton,' said Bridget.

Her husband wasn't listening; the cab had swung to the kerb and already he was opening the door and urging her to step out. He was so eager to reach the station that, taking Bridget by the elbow, he propelled her at a fast trot up the cobbled ramp to the entrance.

'We've plenty of time,' she protested, hampered by the saturated hem of her skirt – though, as it happened, the train had drawn in and the first passengers were hurrying down the platform.

'Are you sure it's right?' asked Bridget, hanging on to his arm, frightened they were in the wrong place.

Alois stood with the nosegay of flowers held ceremoniously in front of him; above the crushed petals his blue eyes stared anxiously ahead. He had lived in Dublin and

Paris and London and had been equally at home in either capital, but at that moment, waiting impatiently in his best clothes beside the ticket gate, searching the approaching faces for that one face in particular, he allowed himself to feel he was a stranger in a strange land. Tears came to his eyes. Consumed with sentiment, he shouldered his way through the crowd and strode on to the platform.

Bridget, unable to follow, ran to the barrier and watched him. For several seconds she lost sight of his broad back, and then the crowd thinned. A woman dressed in furs, supervising the unloading of her luggage, turned to look at Alois as he passed; she took a step after him and hesitated. Bridget waved frantically. She called 'Alois . . . Alois', pushing her arm through the bars of the gate and pointing at the woman who was now walking away. Alois spun round; evidently he hadn't understood, because he was staring at a young man who, half-hidden by an iron column, was peering up at the roof of the train.

Then Bridget witnessed a distressing scene. The young man, suddenly becoming aware of Alois, dodged totally behind the pillar as though for protection – at which Alois sprang forward and seizing him by the collar dragged him into view. An animated conversation began. The young man appeared first to be explaining and then apologising for something; he laid a placating hand on the sleeve of Alois's coat. Alois punched him on the shoulder

11

so forcefully that the young man lost his balance and fell to one knee. The bouquet of flowers tumbled to the platform.

Bridget was alarmed. Only a month ago Alois had spent two nights in the Bridewell for assaulting a drunken seaman in Stanhope Street. The sailor, raucously singing on the pavement below, had disturbed the baby, who woke screaming. It was three o'clock in the morning. Throwing up the sitting-room window, Alois had leaned over the balcony and promised violence if the noise didn't cease. The man sang on. Unwinding the handle from the gramophone and whirling it about his head, Alois had leapt downstairs in his shirt and given chase.

Then as now, Alois seemed immensely threatening. The young man retreated. Alois, apparently losing all control, took a running kick at him. The toe-cap of his boot lifted the welcoming violets into the air; still bunched together by a twist of thread, the flowers sailed over the young man's shoulder and flopped brokenly to the ground. Alois, thwarted, raised his arm menacingly. At that precise moment a passing trolley, laden with baggage, caught the young man a glancing blow on the ankle, and losing his balance for the second time he sprawled helplessly on his back among the suitcases, legs feebly waving as he was borne away down the platform.

Appalled, Bridget shrank against the barrier, watching her husband. She thought she might faint. Brandishing his stick aloft, Alois was now swaying on his feet, convulsed with laughter. People turned to look at him. The young man struggled upright as the trolley neared the end of the platform; jumping clear, he stumbled to the gate and clung to it with both hands. Bridget, separated from him by the iron bars, saw the curve of his high cheek-bone and the bulge of one blue, unhappy eye. She couldn't think why he didn't run for his life. And then Alois, smiling, was standing beside him, thumping him on the back.

'It's my artist brother,' he shouted to Bridget. 'It's bloody Adolf.'

'Pleased to meet you,' said Bridget.

'He took the money,' explained Alois. 'Then he took the excursion.'

'I see,' said Bridget, frowning.

'It takes two to make the bargain,' reminded Alois.

The young man gave up his ticket and passed through the barrier. He was taller than Alois but of a slighter build. He had close-cropped brown hair and a sickly, exhausted face. It appeared that he was worried about a book he had lost, a scholarly work. It was imperative that he find it.

'He was always a great reader,' cried Alois, suddenly proud. Adolf had pressed the book to his breast during the North Sea passage, had held it in his hands throughout the long train journey. Now it was gone; he stared suspiciously over his shoulder at some point above the roof of the locomotive. As it seemed to have been his one item of luggage, Bridget understood his concern.

'We will search up and down,' said Alois kindly. He gave Bridget money for her tram fare home and assured her that the two of them would expect their supper on the table at six-thirty.

'Try not to get heated,' whispered Bridget, fearful that he might do further damage to his relation. She realised finally that Angela wouldn't arrive, that bloody Adolf had come in her place. She was bitterly disappointed. During the day Alois was out touting for business and most nights he worked at the hotel; she was sometimes lonely with only the baby and Mary O'Leary for company. She thought of the best sheets wasted on the brass bed, her mother's bolster case with the initials embroidered at the corner. She'd imagined murmured conversations in the night, womanly talk, small confidences exchanged. Alois had been prepared to give up the bed to his sister; he'd sleep instead on the couch in the sitting room. Obviously it wasn't any longer a suitable arrangement.

Alois took no further notice of Bridget. He was telling his half-brother about safety razors and the fortune that was in it for both of them. A gust of cold wind blew through the station.

Settling her tam o' shanter more firmly on her head, Bridget walked away.

Adolf remained standing by the barrier, sunk in his pockets. His suit was so old a in places the cloth had faded from blue to lilac. staring at each passing face as though expecting someone to recognise him.

3

Once down the slope and into the wintry street, Bridget stood undecided. It was twenty past four by the illuminated clock on the facade of The Seaman's Hotel. Already the lamps were lit on the plateau; in pools of rain the stone lions crouched, waiting to pounce. Mr Meyer would still be in his ground-floor room, strutting back and forth in front of the double windows, knotting his bow-tie beneath his celluloid collar and keeping an eye on the steps. She knew she couldn't go to a tea room because she hadn't the money, and if she stayed out of doors in her leaking boots she would catch pneumonia. Then what would become of darling Pat?

Restricted by such considerations, Bridget walked resentfully along Lime Street towards the tram shelter. It was quite likely she wouldn't see either Alois or his brother again until after the public houses had closed. Alois could talk the hind leg off a donkey, and he wouldn't recollect for one moment the supper drying up in its pot on the fire. Mr Meyer was a great talker too – though he had a terrible habit of leaving things out. He spoke of tragedies, of dilemmas. He was forever alluding to the 'fragile history', as he termed it, of his only child, and never quite making himself plain. Until six months ago the portrait of a young man in the uniform of the White Star Line had hung above the mantelshelf in the front room. The space left by Mr Meyer's son was noticeable; indicating with mournful eyes that luminous oval of flowered paper on the dark wall, Mr Meyer hinted at intolerable suffering. Sometimes Bridget thought it was the powerful nature of Mr Meyer's hints that kept her in thrall. On other occasions, when he came upstairs of an evening for a cup of cocoa and sat with Alois at the hearth, dandling the baby on his knee, she felt she must be a wicked girl; she couldn't take her eyes from Mr Meyer's hand stroking her son's plump limbs in the fire-light.

The tram stop was in Renshaw Street, beyond the Mission building. They were setting up the trestle tables ready for the evening meal of charity soup; the bowls and the wooden spoons were stacked on the mosaic floor of the entrance hall. I've seen it all, thought Bridget – the tables, the spoons splashed with mud, the men with the sacks over their shoulders against the rain. If asked, she was sure she could give an account of it. It was Alois's opinion that she moved through life as though blind. 'Tell me,' he would demand of her from time to time, 'what did you see in the streets, in the washhouse? How many women with grey hair? How many with yellow? Of what colour and pattern were the tiles in the starching room?' But she never could tell him. The expression in his eyes and the tone of his voice silenced her; she stood mute, the words driven from her head. It was the same when, lying in the privacy of their brass bed, he interrogated her in the dark. Is this right? Is that good? The questions, she felt, implied certain set answers that she must always get wrong. Once, before the birth of darling Pat, Alois had won on the National at Aintree and had taken her to Monte Carlo for a holiday. His restaurant in Dale Street had been doing moderately well. He was pleased at the thought of his coming child. Strolling along the road above the bay he had been full of good humour, idly swinging his stick and murmuring on in his expansive way about the vastness of the sky above, the smoothness of the Mediterranean below. She was so accustomed to his chatter that she hardly distinguished his words from the droning of bees in the wild flowers that grew beside the path. Turning to her, he had inquired: 'What colour, do you suppose, is the sea?' 'Why, blue,' she had answered. 'Why, blue,' he had mimicked, and squeezing her arm viciously had shouted: 'The water is a composite of white and blue and green. It is a reflection of the earth and sky, you docile bitch.' For several days after this correction he had ignored her. She sat alone in their hotel room, with its view of the absorbent sea, and looked at her bruised arm in the dressing-table mirror. Had he cared to ask, she could have told Alois, without stammering, that her skin in one particular patch above the elbow was turning black and blue, ringed with a faint tinge of mauve.

Boarding the tram, Bridget was alone in the car save for a woman draped in a shawl and a boy without shoes. His feet swung backwards and forwards above the wooden floor as the tram lurched round the corner past the church and the lighted windows of The Golden Dragon Restaurant. The child was grinning at the sight of a terrified horse pulling a baker's cart whose narrow wheels had caught in the rut of the tramlines. Its nose almost touching the rear of the tram, the horse galloped frantically up the street behind them; a long trail of sparks, showering from the electric cable overhead, rolled along its back. The baker stood upright, his peaked cap falling over one ear, the reins held tight to his chest. Running to the end of the tram, the boy leapt on to the outside stairway and crouched there like a monkey, bouncing up and down and drumming his fists on the rail. Because of the trapped cart the tramdriver accelerated speed. Rattling and throwing up spray on either side like a ferry boat, they breasted the hill to the Infirmary in record time.

There's no help for it, thought Bridget. He'll be sitting now in his dressing-gown, polishing his evening shoes with a scrap of velvet. Resigned to what might happen, she was none the less surprised to find, when alighting from the tram, that she'd missed her usual stop near the dairy and been carried half way down the Boulevard towards the park. She had to walk back along the avenue beneath the dripping chestnut trees. By the time she reached the house she was wet through.

She let herself into the hall and went straightaway to the door of the cellar. Opening it, she peered downwards. It was like the black hole of Calcutta below stairs and there was a terrible smell of damp.

'Have you him safe?' she called.

After a moment Mary O'Leary shouted that the baby was upstairs asleep in his box. He'd had his tea.

Mr Meyer came out of his room and stood in the passage. He was in his stockinged feet and wore a shoe on his hand. He looked inquiringly up and down the hall.

'Where is your sister-in-law?' he asked. 'I don't see her, unless she is very unobtrusive.'

'Ah well,' said Bridget. 'There's been a bit of an alter-cation. It's not what we expected.'

'It is often the case,' said Mr Meyer.

'It's his half-brother that's come instead.'

'The artist brother?' Mr Meyer suggested. 'Adolphus, the lone wolf?'

'That's the one,' said Bridget. 'He walks funny.'

'Like this, perhaps?' Mr Meyer bustled towards her along the passage, arms held stiffly to his sides, the patent-leather shoe pointing at the linoleum.

'No,' Bridget told him. 'More like this', and sliding adroitly past him she minced to the foot of the stairs. She laid her hand on the rail and faced him.

'It's his shoes,' said Mr Meyer. 'Either too large or too small.' He stayed where he was, drooping against the wall. Over his shoulder was draped a brilliant red duster, once a piece of Mary O'Leary's petticoat.

Regretfully Bridget began to climb the stairs. On the half-landing she leaned over the bannister and volunteered: 'The tram ran away with us. I'm all shook up.'

'Your husband was pleased to see him?' asked Mr Meyer. He stared up at her with his head to one side, his grey hair curling against the bright cloth on his shoulder.

'Not that you'd notice,' said Bridget. 'There's been something in the past. Something to do with a letter and his mother. He hasn't a particle of luggage save for an old book, and he's lost that.'

'There's always a letter,' observed Mr Meyer darkly. 'Or a cablegram, or even some words printed small in a newspaper.' He padded silently up the hall to his room and went inside.

The aspidistra on the second-floor landing was dying. It's seen too much, thought Bridget, pushing open the

21

door. Darling Pat was asleep in the bottom drawer of the wardrobe with his fist to his mouth.

She took off her coat before lighting the kerosene lamp on the table. Mr Meyer had installed the electric light, but there was only one bulb hanging from the centre rose of the ceiling and the room was large. She poked the fire into a blaze. Still, there were dark corners and shadows everywhere.

When they had first moved in, Alois had unrolled his precious carpet, salvaged from a previous business invest-ment in a boarding house, and been mortified to see that it looked like a dropped napkin on the expanse of floor-boards. After some consideration he had thought that careful placing of the furniture would make the room appear smaller. Putting the table, the chairs, the mahogany wardrobe, the hat-stand, the couch and the kitchen cupboard on to the carpet, he stood well back at the door and found he now had a large room with a quantity of things piled in the middle and the carpet not showing at all. Depressed, he had left it that way for several months and only gradually shifted the furniture further back, piece by piece, until at last, as though the tide had gone out, the carpet reappeared and the wardrobe, the cupboard, the couch and the hat-stand stood finally washed up against the skirting board. It would never be a room of intimate proportions.

After Bridget had set the table and basted the shoulder

of mutton in its baking tin on the hob of the fire, there was nothing left to occupy her. She wasn't going to move the linen from the bed to the couch, not with Adolf looking as though a good wash would kill him. He'd have to make do with a flannellette sheet and those two blankets Alois had conveniently found abandoned in the corridor of the boat train to Paris.

She knelt down beside the wardrobe and called softly to Pat, nuzzling her little finger into the warm fold of his neck, hoping he would waken so that she could play with him.

'I'm here, Pat,' she crooned. 'Mother's here. Who's Mother's best boy?'

But the baby didn't stir. Mary O'Leary had worn him out.

'I'm here,' Bridget repeated, this time to reassure herself.

She went restlessly to the window and leaned there, listening to the muffled sounds of traffic from the Boulevard; it was so dark outside and so gloomy within, despite the lamp and the flickering fire, that she felt as though she'd fallen down a hole. I'll never be seen again, she thought.

Across the street the darkness yielded suddenly to brilliant light. In the upper room of the public house the gas candelabrum blazed under its shades of tinted glass. She could see the plaster cherub by the door, holding aloft an ornamental lamp. They were stacking the chairs against the windows, ready for the evening's dancing. It was necessary to protect the panes of glass. Last summer an irate dock labourer with throbbing toes, pausing in the middle of the Turkey Trot, had limped in a half-circle about the floor and heaved his partner clean through the window and into the street. The room was inflammatory enough with its scarlet walls and the crimson streamers that dangled from the ceiling, twisting and trembling in the draught. Mr Meyer had told Bridget that the choice of red for the walls was deliberate. It made the people feel hot just looking at it, and so they felt thirsty, and that way they drank more. It was good for business. There was no end to his knowledge. When Alois had first hung pictures in the sitting room – a photograph of his father and three oil paintings of different horses stood in front of some old mountain – Mr Meyer had come upstairs and walking up and down with his chin thrust out pronounced them painted in such-and-such a year after the manner of so-and-so. If he was wrong, Alois hadn't let on. Coming to the portrait in its damaged frame above the hat-stand, Mr Meyer had snapped his fingers. 'That uniform,' he exclaimed. 'A custom official's, if I'm not mistaken. What a stern man . . . a man of iron.' He was certainly in the right of it there, though Bridget wondered how he'd arrived at such a conclusion. To her eyes old man Hitler, with his fat cheeks and that pale fuzz of hair on the top of his head, was the image of darling Pat at six months of age. Save for those grand moustaches he looked for all the world like Pat had when, full of milk and propped on pillows, he'd wobbled in his chair. Mr Meyer was a terrible know-all.

From somewhere downstairs came the murmur of voices, followed by loud laughter. The windows rattled as the front door slammed.

A moment later, a black umbrella bobbed on the pavement below. Reaching the corner, Mr Meyer crossed over to walk beside the church. Violin case dragging along the railings, he squelched into the night.

When he's in the house, thought Bridget, I'm bothered to death. Yet when he's gone, there's regret. She was perpetually surprised that Alois, with his undoubted gift for observation, hadn't noticed the way it was. And how could she tell him? 'It takes two to make the bargain' was one of Alois's favourite expressions. He had said as much to her own father when, outraged by their elopement, he had pursued them to England. Discussing his two incarcerations in prison for theft, once in Dublin and another time in Paris, the details of which Bridget didn't understand, Alois spoke of the special relationship existing between the thief and the man of property. 'They are not separable,' he said. 'One cannot function without the other. It takes two to make the bargain.' Though doubtful about thieving, Bridget was convinced by his argument. She had come from the affectionate arms of her family in Ireland into the passionate arms of her husband. She naturally smiled and clung – Mr Meyer was not entirely to blame. He had proved himself a good friend to Alois. When the restaurant had failed he'd found him night employment as a waiter in the smoking room of the Adelphi Hotel. Half the time it was the left-overs from the kitchens that kept them alive. He had never increased the rent by so much as a farthing. If only his friendly gestures had stopped at Alois.

It had started with a fatherly chuck under the chin and progressed to an all-out embracing of her person. Whenever he had the opportunity, either in the dark lobby or on the second-floor landing, Mr Meyer would seize her and lifting her from the ground hug her to him, laughing as he jiggled her up and down. He didn't attempt to kiss her or to take liberties with her clothing. He merely struggled with her in mid-air, so to speak, chortling throughout. She couldn't think how to break him of the habit. Had she been a child instead of a married woman she supposed she mightn't have known what jigging up and down could lead to. Even so, there was surely an element of danger about the whole procedure. 'Ho ho ho,' he would cry, chin between her breasts, his face turning from ivory to scarlet until, breathing rapidly, he fell into a kind of swoon. She herself experienced a degree of sad excitement. His eyelids fluttered; at first Bridget had thought she was watching him die. His arms slackening, she would slide down him. Cheek to cheek, the aspidistra rocking on its stand, they swayed in the shadows like lovers in a ballroom.

Just then the lights in the dance hall were extinguished. It was now almost totally dark outside. Someone had thrown a brick through the gas-mantle of the lamp on the corner and it had never been replaced. All Bridget could see was the glow of the distant city thrown up against the sky and a glimmer of light touching the pale dome of the church. In the opposite direction the street sloped endlessly downhill, out of sight, past the rows of blackened dwellings, the Brewery and the Home for Incurables, the Soap Works and the Bovril Factory, and ended at the warehouses and the docks. There wasn't a tree growing on it from here to the river.

4

Alois took his brother to a public house on Lime Street. He had no sooner guided the weary traveller through the doors than he sighted a business acquaintance he was anxious to avoid. Taking Adolf by the arm and murmuring vaguely that the place was too crowded for comfort, he bundled him on to the pavement again. Adolf had caught a brief glimpse of the almost empty interior and felt there was something sinister in their hasty retreat. Drenched with rain and shivering, he allowed himself to be propelled further along the street. He was bewildered by the crowds that marched shoulder to shoulder in either direction, jostling and bumping into one another. He thought wildly that he must have stumbled into a demonstration, an uprising of some kind. At one moment he was forced into the gutter and almost run down by a brewer's cart pulled by a horse the size of an elephant. Rosettes in its harness and water streaming off its massive haunches, the animal thundered past him. He had never seen such a horse. Trembling, he clung to Alois's arm and was dragged into a public house on the next corner.

Here he sat at a little round table beside a panelled partition with a screen of glass above, elaborately cut and patterned. Normally he detested spirits, but now his whole body was shuddering with cold and fatigue. His teeth chattering against the rim of the glass, he drank his measure of gin at one gulp.

Alois began immediately to talk about himself and his ambitions for the future. He made no apologies for claiming to have been the youngest as well as the most popular under-manager ever employed by the Ritz Hotel in Paris. He knew his own worth. When the band struck up and the diners rose from their tables, the women couldn't resist bumping into him. Many a time, one lady or another, foxtrotting across the polished floor, feathers trembling in her head-dress, had glanced over the shoulder of her partner and flashed him messages with her eyes. His progress in London had been equally splendid . . . The people he had met . . . And as for Liverpool, though he said it himself, he had done so well that within six months of arriving in the city he had bought his own hotel and later a restaurant. Not for the riff-raff, of course . . . his customers had mainly consisted of shipping kings and cotton magnates . . . the real swells. But his undoubted ability at catering was as nothing compared with his flair for commerce. His superior knowledge of the market concerned couldn't fail to build up an enterprise that would eventually be worth millions. In no time at all it would become an empire. If only he had the trifling funds necessary to launch such a venture.

Adolf was bemused. The gin had gone to his head and he felt as though he was on the channel steamer again, rising and sinking with the waves.

'In a while,' Alois prophesied, 'no one will think of using anything else. In my capacity as chief salesman for the whole of the North West, I'm in a position to judge. I have contacts in Bradford . . . in Manchester. You name the big names . . . I know them.'

Adolf knew no names. He thought he had missed some important turn in the conversation. They seemed to have abandoned the frivolous area of the dance floor in favour of big business. 'Once,' he confided, 'I had the idea of enclosing old banknotes in celluloid, thus making them more durable. Of course one would have to make them smaller.'

'Such a smooth shave,' Alois said. 'Such a gentle action against the skin. Take my word for it, they're all the rage.'

'Another time,' remembered Adolf, 'I had the notion that there was a great deal of money to be made out of filling old tins with paste and selling them to shopkeepers. In Vienna during the winter the windows freeze over. You can't see the goods displayed.'

'Surely,' Alois objected, 'the paste would be as bad as the frost.'

'It was never put to the test,' said Adolf. He was temporarily blinded. There were so many points of light in the room, so many glittering reflections – he could hardly distinguish his brother. It wasn't, in any case, a recognisable face. Alois had left home when Adolf was nine years old. There seemed little connection between that thin, poorly complexioned youth of sixteen and the somewhat stout and prosperous man who sat opposite, obsessed with razor blades.

Alois insisted on divulging his plans for trade expansion. He spoke of freight trains and cargo boats and a shrinking world. In time, God willing, it could be more economical to finance one's own railroad. 'It'll be simple for me,' he reasoned. 'Child's play. I have after all numerous contacts in Paris and in Munich . . . and with Angela so conveniently situated in Linz . . .' He broke off abruptly and glared across the table.

Adolf was almost asleep. He was so relaxed, head lolling against the padded back of the seat, that he felt his limbs were drifting away from his body; his mouth had fallen open. Steam began to rise from his damp clothing. Somewhere, long ago he had leapt from the barn loft into the stack below . . . Just such a stifling scent of dried clover rose to engulf him as he drowned in the colourless hay.

31

A violent rocking of the table and a hand at his throat jerked him into consciousness. He opened his eyes to find Alois looming over him, demanding to know how he'd wheedled the money out of Angela.

'What money?' he asked, shocked. He thought his brother was still thinking in terms of millions.

'My money,' shouted Alois. 'The money I sent Angela for her ticket.' He gripped the front of Adolf's shirt and twisted it so severely that its wearer was in danger of being asphyxiated.

'I didn't wheedle,' cried Adolf. 'She gave it to me freely. She said she couldn't leave the children.' Already the skin across his cheek-bones was growing mottled. He felt choked, not by the pressure of his brother's fingers but by hatred. The room grew dark before his eyes; he heard the blood pounding in his ears.

Alois released him and sat back angrily in his chair. Across his forehead, where the band of his elegant hat had pressed, beads of perspiration gathered. He muttered sullenly, 'You had no right.'

Adolf struggled to pull himself together, to utter some remark that would show how unaffected he was. He longed to shrug his shoulders indifferently, to smile mockingly. He could manage none of these pretences. He stared into the florid face of Alois and scowled in return. For a moment there came to him an image of his father holding his brother by the neck against a walnut tree and beating him with a leather strap until he fainted. The family dog ran round and round the tree, barking. Seizing him too by the scruff of the neck, Father struck him repeatedly. Released, the animal crawled on its belly in the grass and wet itself.

'You had no right,' repeated Alois, mopping his brow with a handkerchief. 'It was my money.'

'I shall repay it instantly,' shouted Adolf, foolishly proud.

Fortunately, while he was thrusting his hands deep into his empty pockets, a man carrying a violin case approached the table. Alois started up and greeted him warmly. He wanted the man to sit down. He was all smiles again.

'I came merely to welcome Adolphus,' said the stranger. 'I mean no permanent intrusion.' He stood with his hand resting on Alois's shoulder.

Adolf sat bolt upright, his collar askew and a button gone from his shirt. His worst fears were confirmed. Though the official scrutinising him, dressed in black from head to foot like an undertaker, bore no resemblance either to the man on the boat or to the improbable figure on the balcony of the tower, he had no doubt that they were in collusion. He waited, legs trembling beneath the shining surface of the table, expecting at any moment to be arrested.

And yet, the stranger's expression wasn't altogether

hostile. Biding his time, he studied Adolf carefully, as if not entirely sure he was the one.

Something about the man was peculiarly familiar. Adolf couldn't help but think of his two closest acquaintances in Vienna, Josef Neumann and Jakob Altenburg. At certain angles, seen through the window of a café or in profile on the street, Josef appeared haughty, almost contemptuous. This impression was due to the mask-like composure of his features and had little to do with the shape of his nose or the fullness of his lips. It was as though, rather in the manner of the leopard and its spots, he had inherited from others before him a uniformity that enabled him to move undetected through the surrounding jungle. But suddenly, his attention drawn by a rapping on the glass or the calling of his name, he would turn and smile like a woman, warmly and seductively, his whole face transformed. Then it was perfectly plain to which species he belonged.

'Journeys,' said the man, 'are often uncomfortable. Sometimes one's feet hurt abominably.'

Adolf stared.

'Unless one can afford to travel in style,' added the man.

'He can't afford to travel at all,' Alois said. He winked maliciously. 'These struggling artists never have a half-penny.'

Adolf began another futile search of his pockets. He

said bitterly, 'I'm a painter of postcards. It isn't the same thing.' He hated being referred to as an artist, struggling or otherwise. Since his last and final rejection by the Academy of Fine Arts in Vienna, he preferred to think of himself as a student. He yawned, both from tiredness and a sense of failure.

'If it was me,' the man said, 'I would go wherever I was going and lie down and close my eyes. For a time I would hear noises in my head. Am I right?'

Adolf pursed his lips and wouldn't reply. He thought he was being tricked into some admission. He gazed fixedly at the far wall and the painting of a black ship that sailed across a cracked and varnished sea.

'When I was a young boy,' the fiddle-player recollected, 'my mother feared I had the sleeping sickness. I could stay in bed from dawn till dusk. No effort at all. My body burned with activity, but my mind slumbered. Now . . . it is the other way round. I wake in the night like an infant . . . I nibble slices of sausage as though my life depended on it . . . I pace up and down like a sentry though there is nothing left to guard. My body is tired out but the mind refuses to rest.'

At this, Adolf couldn't resist glancing upwards. The man smiled. His large, melancholy eyes shone with dreadful tenderness.

Adolf was greatly affected by the quality of this smile. He had been unnaturally controlled for many hours. The long train journey full of unfathomable alarms, Alois's boisterous greeting and his vulgar talk of intrigues and empires had held him in a state of perpetual suspense, of tension. He had been in the position of the hunter who, sighting his prey when least expected, knows that the slightest sign of agitation will produce a stench of fear and bring the beast with outstretched claws bounding towards him. Now, he could run to that equal beside the camp-fire and admit he had come face to face with death.

'It's true,' he stammered, 'I can't stop thinking.' He realised that the man so kindly regarding him was unlike either Neumann or Jakob Altenburg. There was someone else whom he resembled, some earlier figure who carried not a violin case but a Gladstone bag containing wads of gauze and a bottle of iodoform. It was the doctor who had attended his mother when she was dying of cancer and who had comforted him when, the life gone from her, she lay with a rosary piously tangled in her fingers. 'My dear boy,' Dr Bloch had promised, 'in time you will get over it. Believe me.'

One doesn't lose all sense of judgment, thought Adolf, after a single glass of spirits. Here at last was an individual of the same calibre as himself, a human being of sensitivity, one who could speak of important matters, of things that nourished the soul.

The man, turning to Alois, began to talk in English.

Adolf watched their faces and listened to the strange sounds. All the while he was conscious that the eyes of the fiddler still glowed with that mournful expression of sweet concern.

'Do you want me to try for cutlets tonight, or would you prefer the fish? You have the mutton, don't forget.'

'Fish,' replied Alois. 'Peaches too, if it could be managed.'

'It can be managed.' Looking at Adolf, the stranger lifted his violin case in the air and tapped it significantly.

'I don't play an instrument,' confessed Adolf. 'I never had the opportunity. But I love music – Wagner in particular.'

'We have a very fine concert hall,' the man told him. 'You must go there.' Assuring Adolf that they would meet presently, he raised his black felt hat in a polite gesture of farewell and threaded his way between the tables to the door.

'You were bought a piano by Mother,' said Alois. 'According to Angela it was an expensive model. And you had lessons.'

'Very few,' Adolf said sharply. 'Later, the piano was sold. Angela and Paula shared the money.'

Feeling perhaps that he had spoken unfairly, Alois offered to buy his brother another drink. Adolf shook his head primly.

'Just one more,' persisted Alois. 'I don't mind about

the money. You can pay me back when you're on your feet.'

'I don't approve of spirits,' said Adolf, his face growing more pinched and disapproving than ever.

'Goddammit,' cried Alois, exasperated. 'I can't stand a man who doesn't drink', and manoeuvring himself from his chair he strode angrily away.

5

Adolf sprawled listlessly against the partition. Now that the musician had gone, doubts began to assail him. Had there been an implied threat behind the words 'We shall meet again'? Why the ferocious insistence that he should visit the concert hall? And those noises he might hear in his head – were they whispered injunctions to give himself up, or the more ominous sound of military boots tramping towards him? What was the old Jew getting at with his maudlin anecdotes of lazy adolescence, his tragic expression, that bamboozling air of feigned and moist compassion? There was nowhere he could hide and no one he could turn to for help. He supposed his half-brother had deserted him. He slumped deeper in his chair, horribly awake, and stared at the band of grey silk that encircled the crown of Alois's splendid and abandoned hat.

However, after only a few minutes absence at the bar,

Alois returned and seated himself once more behind the table. Adolf was immensely relieved, but he said nothing.

'What's the time?' asked Alois, although he knew already. He could think of no other way of ending the unfriendly silence.

Adolf replied sullenly that he hadn't any idea, so sullenly that his brother couldn't resist stating the obvious. 'You haven't a watch.'

'I have no time for watches.'

'You have no hat either. And no overcoat.'

Adolf ignored him. He was filled with contempt for those outward signs of Alois's success – his fat cheeks, his thin elegant cane that stood propped against the wall, those links of heavy silver that hung in a glittering loop from button-hole to inside vest.

'What's that disagreeable smell?' demanded Alois wrinkling his fleshy nose in distaste.

Offended, Adolf crouched there, holding his breath as though to deny the existence of any odour. He imagined that his portly relation, dressed in layers of expensive cloth, had never suffered the humiliation of poverty. While Alois had been swaggering through the foyers of swanky hotels, ogling women between the potted palms, he himself, wearing this same suit of clothes, had slept on a bench in the Prater and sometimes, in wet weather, under the arches of the Rotunda. When winter came and the first fall of snow, fearing he might freeze to death he had trudged the two and a half miles to Meidling on the outskirts of Vienna and queued for admittance at the Asyl für Obdachlose. Once inside he had been interrogated and his particulars written down. He had no job, no address, no qualifications and he refused to admit to any religious beliefs. His entire life, with its small triumphs and disasters, its boundless hopes and aspirations for the future, was condensed to a few words scrawled on a piece of grey paper the size of a visiting card. This puny dossier was no sooner completed than it was stamped with a row of figures that effectively obliterated his name and date of birth. For some reason he had been terrified at the sight of those impersonal digits. He longed to make a scene, to insist they brand these same numbers on his forehead or his wrist, thus drawing attention to their own lack of humanity. But he hadn't the courage, and besides from the corridors beyond had come a delicious aroma of potato soup. At that moment he was no longer a man, merely a huge mouth that gushed with saliva. Subdued and listed as 848763/Male, he was led to a large room and told to undress. The ceiling was covered in intricate lengths of piping and the floor was tiled. Here he bathed in public and later stood with a square of towelling held modestly in front of him while his clothes were disinfected. When they were returned to him, the armpits of his jacket and the crotch of his threadbare trousers had

41

turned a delicate shade of lilac. Periodically over the last three years he had undergone the same demeaning ritual in various other institutions. He was now like a walking weather-vane – the least hint of dampness in the air and an unmistakable reek of lysol instantly emanated from him.

'I may have an overcoat that would fit you,' said Alois, and added: 'It's hardly in my best interests to be seen with someone so shabbily dressed as yourself.' He was looking down as he spoke, tapping the rim of his glass with the edge of his wedding ring.

Until that moment Adolf had been huddling, metaphorically, on some ledge above an abyss. Several times he had felt himself swaying. Now, with that brutal offer of second-hand finery, Alois kicked him into the depths. Falling, he grasped at the table and tilted it towards him. The glass slid from beneath Alois's fingers; he looked up and was startled by the absurd expression of rage on Adolf's face. He was holding his head at a curious angle as though an invisible hand was pulling his hair out by the roots and sneering so ferociously it was almost comical. As he stared dumbfounded, Adolf began to snarl like a cornered fox.

'Pull yourself together,' said Alois, embarrassed. He shifted his chair further round the table, endeavouring to screen this extraordinary sight from the rest of the room. He had a fair temper himself, as he would be the first to admit, but he was staggered by this rather effeminate display of snickering frenzy. Some instinct prevented him from slapping his hysterical brother across the cheek.

Adolf started to shout incoherently. Alois had swelled to such vast proportions that his mouth, beneath those hateful and beautifully trimmed moustaches, was capable of devouring him. He half raised his fist, prepared to burst those pink ballooning cheeks.

Just then Alois, who had some experience of horses, realising that Adolf was ready to buck violently, smashing the glass panels to smithereens in the process, took out his handkerchief and began to murmur 'Steady, whoa, steady' over and over again. He managed eventually to slip an arm about his brother's hunched and trembling shoulders. Twice Adolf, ranting incomprehensibly about vermin and redskins and men with beards, broke away from him. But he was wearing himself out. At last he allowed Alois, still uttering those little clucking noises of motherly firmness, to dab at his lower lip which was bleeding quite copiously from the constant snapping of his agitated jaws. Rising, and thinking glumly that this was yet another public house he wouldn't care to show his face in for some time, Alois steered him through a dozen smirking onlookers to the door.

6

Adolf's behaviour in the street was equally wayward. He shied at the approaching tram car and refused to board it. Wheeling, he was off at a fast trot. Fearing a scandal might jeopardise his future business schemes, Alois pursued him and bundled him into a cab. During the brief journey Adolf complained that he could hear someone playing a violin. He sat with his hands clapped over his ears, swinging his head backwards and forwards.

On the pavement outside the house he moaned about pianos and saxophones. He said the street throbbed to the beat of Dixieland jazz.

'I thought you liked music?' said Alois, aggrieved.

Once upstairs, he explained to Bridget that their guest was exhausted.

'Is that so?' said Bridget, thinking that if it were true then Adolf had a queer way of showing it. He was walking round and round the room so rapidly that she grew dizzy just watching him. The pallor of his skin and the flecks of blood on his torn shirt alarmed her. 'I told you not to get in a paddy,' she scolded. 'Look at the state of him.'

'I've been like a lamb,' Alois retorted. 'A lesser man would have strangled him. He's had some sort of fit.'

'A fit?' she cried, and her hands shook as she served the supper.

Conversation at the table wasn't as she'd imagined. No one complimented her on her cooking or asked how many teeth the baby had. Adolf took exception to the photograph of his father above the hat-stand. He said the old man's ugly face was putting him off his food. Alois told him to keep a civil tongue in his head. Raising his fork threateningly in the air, he dripped gravy on the nice white cloth. At which Bridget, voluble with embarrassment, recounted the saga of the runaway cart with its wheels caught in the tramlines.

'The old fella driving the cart,' she said, 'was clinging on for dear life. He was losing his hat.' She lifted her hands to touch her auburn hair.

In the middle of this description Adolf turned to Alois and demanded to know what she was saying. Impatiently Alois began the story again. Half-way through, Adolf leapt up from the table and spun round and round with knees bent and his arms held out like wings. The starched napkin tucked into his collar hung stiff as a board over his wretched shirt.

'God bless us,' cried Bridget, watching his frantic caper-ings on the pink carpet. His white face reminded her of the urchin on the tram. Was it mirth or belly pains that gripped him?

'He's off again,' said Alois, rising from his chair. He pulled the sofa nearer the fire and taking Adolf by the arm laid him forcibly down and covered him with the plaid blankets.

'I've had enough,' he told Bridget. 'I'm going out.'

'Don't leave me,' she pleaded.

'He's not dangerous,' Alois said. 'The silly beggar thinks someone's stolen his cap. Shut yourself in the bedroom if you're worried.'

He turned out the electric light and picked up his coat and walking stick.

'Is it catching?' Bridget asked, concerned for darling Pat. But with a shrug of his shoulders Alois left her and went running down the stairs. It occurred to him that it had been the most regrettable action of his life to send money to his sister in Linz.

7

For five days and nights Adolf lay almost continuously on the sofa in the front room. He had only to stumble upstairs to the lavatory on the third-floor landing and back again to fall immediately insensible among the crumpled blankets. He slept in his clothes and ate nothing apart from a plate of mutton broth on the third day. The sofa, which for his greater comfort had originally been placed close to the banked-up fire, was dragged back by Alois and reversed so that it faced the wall and hid the sleeper from view.

It wasn't a happy time for Bridget. She felt she was an intruder in her own home, compelled to walk on tiptoe, obliged to keep the baby from making too much noise. She didn't want them both to be murdered while Alois was out selling his safety razors. She fled downstairs to the basement, looking for sympathy from Mary O'Leary.

Mary was sixty-five years old and Russian. Bridget

supposed she was Mr Meyer's maid-of-all-work. She did his washing and she certainly cooked him a dinner every Sunday at around four o'clock. At half-past three Meyer prudently opened both the lobby doors and the door on to the street in preparation for the fumes that would soon engulf the house from cellar to attic. Sometimes Mary scrubbed the front steps, and now and then she was to be seen on her massive knees in the hall, rubbing the oil-cloth with a dry rag. Mostly she stayed below stairs and gave her full attention to the fire, careful never to let it go out. She stood at her post like an eccentric stoker, a shovel always by her side, wrestling hourly with the intricate series of flues and dampers that regulated the ancient range. Clamped on her grey head was a poke bonnet she had worn as a girl, its gaudy ribbons long since frazzled up into two charred knots that dangled on either side of her fiercely burning cheeks.

The basement was undoubtedly the warmest room in the house, though the underground spring that ran beneath the sloping street overflowed from time to time and flooded in knee-high over the stone-flagged floor. With its low ceiling, its gas chandelier of cast iron hanging like a lump of rock above the scrubbed table, the room had a dignity according to Mr Meyer that the rest of the premises lacked, having been torn apart and reno-vated and partitioned by a succession of ignorant land-lords. Bridget herself thought it was a desperate hole to live in. There were rats leaping, supple as ferrets, through the coal cellar and strange vegetable growths sprouting on the damp walls.

Mary O'Leary was standing at the table manhandling half a dozen of Mr Meyer's soiled and celluloid shirt fronts. She listened to Bridget's complaints.

'First he had no luggage,' Bridget said. 'And now it turns out he was robbed every step of the way. Books and clothing and things. He hasn't even a change of shirt, and his shoes are worn through. He talks in his sleep. He has bad dreams.'

'Great God,' muttered Mary O'Leary, scraping at the collars with the worn heel of her scrubbing brush.

'. . . He said he spent a fortune on some medicine that made his mother die. It stained her yellow and closed her throat.'

'It's a wonder he didn't choke saying it,' Mary O'Leary cried.

'It was Alois that said it,' admitted Bridget. 'I don't know what the truth is, but it can't be good for the baby.'

'What does he look like?' asked Mary, referring to the guest with nightmares. She wasn't being nosey. Two months after her fortieth birthday, while working as a skivvy for her Uncle Reub in his watch-menders shop on Brownlow Hill, she had been approached by an Irishman, taken to a twopenny hop, briefly courted and unexpectedly married. On her wedding night her husband had protested that she was both old and hairy, and had departed in the morning, never to be seen again. Mary was no longer sure of the size of him or what colour his eyes had been or his hair, but she was still puzzled by his disappearance and far from convinced that his was a permanent absence. Often when Mr Meyer brought home friends she would steam up the hall and ask 'Is it him?', as though twenty-five years was yesterday and the elusive O'Leary had merely popped round the corner for a twist of tobacco.

'He's not tall,' said Bridget. 'But then I've hardly seen him on his feet. He has very blue eyes. His head's shaved.'

'How old?' demanded Mary O'Leary.

'Twenty-three,' Bridget said. 'Alois is worried about his papers. He doesn't think they're in order.' She didn't care to tell Mary that while his brother slept Alois had already rifled his pockets and found his passport incorrect.

'He's an artist,' said Mary O'Leary. 'Meyer told me. He said they don't always do what's convenient.'

Bridget didn't know what to think. Alois was very contradictory in his statements. In the past he had called Adolf a gifted architect, a scholar, a man of special talents. His opinion was based on memories of his half-brother as a boy and information given him by his sister Angela. Why, when Angela's husband had died leaving her with young children to support and Alois's sister Paula to look after, Adolf had voluntarily surrendered the small pension left to him by old man Hitler and made it over to Angela. He was generous, clever and someone with a future. Now however, with Adolf slumbering in the actual heart of his living room, Alois fumed that he was a dead weight, a thief, that he had always been spoilt. In order to prise the money out of him Angela had been forced to take him to court. He had broken his mother's heart and wiped his bum with his report card from the Realschule.

'It's certainly inconvenient,' Bridget said, 'to have him lying there all day long. I don't know where to put myself.'

Mary O'Leary wanted to know if she could take a peep at him. Just to see what manner of person he was. She shovelled more coal on to the fire to make sure it wouldn't die on her while her back was turned.

'There's not much of him visible,' said Bridget. 'He's facing the wall and he keeps his head under the blankets.'

'Great God,' whispered Mary O'Leary. 'That you should have a corpse on your hands.' Elbows moving like pistons, she mounted the stairs to the second floor.

'Is he all right?' breathed Bridget. Adolf lay on his back with his arms folded over his face. Still attached to his frayed collar, her napkin, now limp and creased, rose and gently fell.

'I have seen this before,' said Mary O'Leary. 'The wife of my Uncle Reub lay just so for many years. Now and then she called piteously for her Mammy.' She stared thoughtfully down at the pole-axed visitor. 'Possibly a sudden shock will bring him back.' And she waved her arms above the sofa and emitted several guttural shouts as though she was engaged in riddling the boiler.

Darling Pat, lying peacefully asleep in the wardrobe drawer, woke and began to cry loudly.

Adolf slept on.

'Perhaps a bucket of water would do more good,' observed Mary O'Leary.

'Years,' wailed Bridget tearfully, picking up the baby and patting his back. 'I can't stand another day.' If she hadn't alienated her mother's heart by running off in the first place, she might have packed her bags and taken the next boat home to Dublin.

'At least you know where he is,' said Mary O'Leary.

8

Each time Adolf opened his eyes, huge shadows drifted above him. He knew there was a party in progress; he distinctly heard music and people singing. At one moment, despairing of ever persuading him to dance, they dragged him horizontally across the floor. A series of images flickered in front of him – a girl in a cream blouse, an old woman waving her arms in anguish, a man with hair the colour of silver, wagging a solemn finger – and Alois, holding a wine glass up to the goose-necked lamp on the wall, was talking about the day before yesterday: '. . . Of course Mother took his part . . . A bruise the size of an egg on my left temple . . . She said he would never have gone into the cemetery unless I led him . . .'

The unfairness of this conversation roused Adolf. He remembered quite clearly how he had pulled back and refused to enter the cemetery. He didn't want to look directly at Edwin's grave – it was bad enough seeing that small grey cross from the window of his bedroom. He struggled upright, determined to call Alois a liar, and found he was standing in a room facing towards a door inset with a panel of stained glass. There were no steps outside, only a drop to a small and azure blue backyard. In the middle of the yard stood a tall youth brandishing a chopper above the head of a child who crouched in the blue dirt on blackberry-coloured knees.

The room was empty save for a rusted bath-tub in the corner; above it, riveted precariously to the wall, sagged an elaborate cylinder made of copper. Draped over the edge of the tub was a little red towel, scarlet as a poppy, so bright that Adolf stared at it for a long time thinking what a nice painting it would make – the towel, the cylinder, the panes of blue glass set in the door leading nowhere.

Suddenly he realised he was being watched, knowingly, by a man in a stained cravat who was standing on a wooden crate and urinating. White with disgust Adolf ran down the dark stairs, unsettling the aspidistra on its rickety pedestal, and glimpsed out of the corner of his eye the man with silvery hair, now dwarfed by the girl in the cream blouse who towered above him in some miraculous way as they waltzed sluggishly about the landing.

Alois was still talking, waggling the stem of his glass so close to Adolf's face that it seemed he intended to grind it into splinters up his nostrils: '. . . Three had died, don't forget . . . Gustav and Ida in infancy . . . Edwin at six of the measles . . . As mere stepchildren Angela and I didn't get a look in . . .'

Adolf lay down and folded his arms over his eyes. Somebody was crying. An enormous tear splashed on to his mouth and saturated his chest.

9

Bridget waited at a safe distance while her husband emptied the jug of water over the sofa. Should a fight break out she was ready to tell Alois she had stood enough and was off to stay with her cousin Bernadette in Knotty Ash.

Adolf woke. He sat up and, like a swimmer breasting a wave, hung gasping over the back of the sofa.

'Right,' said Alois. 'There's a tap on the landing and a mirror in the lavatory upstairs. I'll leave you my razor. When I return I expect to find you washed and shaved and moving about. You'll lose the use of your limbs if you lie there much longer. Do you hear?'

'Yes,' said Adolf. Surely, he thought, Alois was talking with his tongue in his cheek – had he forgotten the beatings he himself had taken as a boy for not washing his neck properly, for not getting up promptly enough from his bed in the morning? How exactly like old man Hitler he sounded. He glanced at the wall half-expecting to see those lips, in the photograph above the hat-stand, opening and closing.

'Now that you've come,' Alois continued, 'you might as well explore the city. No point in wasting the money you've already squandered on the ticket. But you'll need clothes. If you were living next door with the riff-raff it wouldn't matter. This however is a respectable house and you'll only draw attention to yourself dressed the way you are.' He looked meaningfully at Adolf. 'We don't want that, do we? Not the way things stand.'

'No,' said Adolf, though he wasn't entirely sure what Alois was driving at.

'There's nothing of mine that will fit, but I'll have a word with Meyer.' Alois took out his pocket watch and studied it. He was still wearing his gloves and his expensive top-coat. 'It's ten o'clock,' he told Adolf. 'I want you on your feet in half an hour.'

Adolf looked at the windows to see if it was night or day. It was hard to tell; the sky outside was grey as slate. It had stopped raining.

'Thank you,' he said.

He gave a small submissive smile. He was thinking that until he had thought out why he was here and what he intended to do once he knew, there was no harm in appearing to be grateful. Alois was an open book to him. For all his blustering talk, his apparent firmness, he was goodnatured, tolerant and so completely without depth, that it was impossible for him to sustain rancour for longer than half an hour at the most.

Bridget went on to the landing with her husband. He was delighted at having dealt with Adolf so satisfactorily. He kissed Bridget's cheek and laid a gloved hand on her breast. She drew instantly away, worried that Mr Meyer might be lurking round the bend of the stairs – she didn't want him inflamed beyond reason with only the weary Adolf left to protect her. She sensed that her withdrawal had annoyed Alois; he had taken it for revulsion. She thought sadly that it was on such foolish misunderstandings that lives floundered and love went flying out of the window. But then his love for her, she well knew, had flown long ago and he would jump at the excuse to skedaddle.

Alois's irritation was momentary. Later in the day he had an important appointment with a manufacturer from Sheffield. He was convinced that it would lead to a substantial commission.

'We won't have any more trouble from him,' he said, nodding in the direction of the front room. 'Obviously he responds to authority.' He descended the stairs two at a time, filled with optimism.

Bridget gave her brother-in-law a basin and a towel. She showed him the tap on the landing and the sink in the alcove. She said hesitatingly: 'I'd wash your shirt, but there's nothing you could wear in the meantime but an old blouse of mine. Alois is very fussy about lending his clothes.'

He looked at her blankly. Her knowledge of German was poor and her accent atrocious: it took a little time for him to fathom what she meant.

'It doesn't matter,' he said. 'Please don't trouble yourself. Perhaps there is a muffler I could borrow.'

She found it equally difficult to understand him. He spoke differently from Alois. 'No,' she said, hoping that was the right answer.

When Adolf returned with the basin he was bleeding from several minute cuts on the chin. He flung the safety razor contemptuously on to the table. Now that his face was clean and the stubble gone from his jaw he appeared younger and more fatigued than ever. Watching him sidle across the room, Bridget nearly burst out laughing. She wasn't an unkind girl, but with that funny walk and in his ridiculously shrunken jacket he reminded her of one of the broker's men in a pantomine.

'Food,' she said. 'You'll need some food.'

She settled the coals and put the pot on to heat. While she stood there minding the soup she was thinking how like Alois he was and yet how different. Alois was flamboyant and confident, plumped out with self-regard. The young man standing at the window was painfully thin and his shoulders were rounded. He had a long bony face and a pointed nose. Unless she turned him to the light and deliberately stared into those bright blue eyes she had no means of telling why, though of the same colour and shape as Alois's, they were so utterly dissimilar in expression. Perhaps Adolf took after his mother.

Despite his long rest, Adolf felt tired and weak. There was no strength in his legs and his heart was behaving strangely. Just walking from the door to the window had caused it to leap in his breast in a painful flutter of beats that left him sick and giddy. He clung to the window-frame – the row of black houses on the grey street tilted suddenly and slid towards the leaden grey of the sky.

'Are you all right?' asked Bridget. He didn't look it. He hadn't a speck of colour in his face and he was buckling at the knees.

'Quite all right,' said Adolf, and forcing himself to stand upright he limped to the sofa and made a feeble attempt to straighten its wrinkled cover. He punched the cushions into shape and picked up the blankets.

'No,' cried Bridget, taking them from him. 'It's not necessary.' She thought there was no sense folding them when possibly it was fumigation they required.

Adolf sat at the table and found himself facing the photograph of his father. He moved immediately.

'When I was on the landing,' he said, 'I thought I heard shouts. And then there was a crash as if something fell.'

'You heard right,' Bridget said. 'It's them next door.

They'll be pulling up the floorboards to burn on the fire. They're nothing but a heap of savages.' Then, dimly remembering how Mr Meyer had explained to her that it wasn't the fault of the poor if they were pig-ignorant but due to the greed of the ruling classes or someone like that, she added: 'The woman on the second floor's had nineteen children and there's sixteen of them in one room, hacking the place to bits. The daddy's a Portuguese man and she's an albino. You know – she's got pink, eyes and no lashes to speak of. Only the other day one of them ran amok with an axe. The family underneath are scared for their lives.'

Adolf had understood little of Bridget's conversation. He noticed that she had a snub nose and a wide, rather brutal mouth. Standing there, waving that wooden spoon in the air, he thought she lacked refinement. His ideal woman, the divine Stefanie with whom he had fallen in love in Vienna, had been tall with hair as pale as glass.

While he was drinking his soup a man's voice from somewhere outside on the stairs called Bridget's name.

She sat as if turned to stone, the blood draining from her face.

Adolf now realised that the vulgar patches of scarlet on her cheeks he had mistaken for rouge were in fact clusters of freckles, fading as he watched. Her eyes too were flecked with gold. 'Is it bad news?' he asked, but she rose from the table and left him without a word.

When she returned some moments later, apple-cheeked as ever, she wouldn't look at him directly. 'Mr Meyer,' she said, speaking to the wall, 'is waiting downstairs to see you.'

Adolf remained in his chair, baffled.

'Don't you remember?' asked Bridget. 'You met him the night you arrived. He's the landlord.' She grew impatient. 'The man with the violin,' she shouted, tucking in her chin and miming the scraping of a bow across strings. 'The clever one . . .'

Now Adolf knew whom she meant. Instantly he felt restored to health. Some of his so-called friends had been dreadful fools. The banality of their thoughts had appalled him. When talking to them he was oppressed by the feeling he mouthed on the other side of a thick wall, unheard, unseen. He had read that great artists, great people, felt exactly as he did, but it wasn't much comfort. Now some instinct told him everything would be different. He forgot entirely his previous mistrust of the fiddler. He jumped up from the table, eyes shining, as though he was about to meet an old and valued comrade. But first he must wash up the dish and the spoon he had used.

'Leave them,' Bridget said curtly.

He thought he had offended her in some way. 'Thank you for the meal,' he said. 'I greatly appreciated it.'

She snatched up his plate and turned her back on him before the words were out of his mouth.

Later, Bridget went down to the basement to ask Mary O'Leary if she had any material suitable to be made into a shirt. She wanted to make amends to Adolf for having snapped at him earlier. It wasn't fair to take it out on the poor young fellow just because she grew agitated whenever Meyer gave her so much as the time of day. She told Mary she didn't mind what stuff it was. Anything at all would do. An old sheet perhaps.

'What's that supposed to mean?' asked Mary O'Leary. 'Old sheets is all we have, and you're not cutting them into pieces.'

In the end she fished out a length of brown linen shut in a battered suitcase in the coal cellar.

'Who does that belong to when it's at home?' said Bridget.

Mary O'Leary explained that the gentleman in the attic had left it with her for safekeeping fourteen years ago.

'Brown?' Bridget said dubiously. 'It's an odd colour for a shirt.'

'Get away,' scoffed Mary O'Leary. 'The one he's wearing is like a rag the doggie brought in.'

She beat the material with her hand to let out the dust. There was only a smattering of mildew along the creases.

10

Had the fiddler lived in tawdry surroundings, in a room filled with cheap knick-knacks and hung with second-rate paintings of the sort Alois admired, Adolf was prepared to tell himself it didn't matter. A man, he felt, should be judged by his intellect not his possessions. As it happened, Meyer's apartment had a grandeur that might have been oppressive but for the fact that each time the door was opened or closed quantities of plaster fell from the ceiling and clung like snow to every available surface. The furniture, old and dark, monumental in size, was liberally sprinkled with flakes of white, as were the windowsills. The effect was festive. Pinned above the fireplace was a collection of photographs cut from newspapers, showing workmen rioting, the *Titanic* on her maiden voyage, and a woman wearing an agonised expression holding a bundle in her arms. Propped against the straddle-legged clock on the mantelpiece was a faded daguerrotype of a young man with insolently staring eyes. Along the length of one wall stood an immense glass-fronted bookcase.

That first morning, seeing Adolf gazing hungrily at those volumes behind the glass, Meyer had said: 'Come here whenever you like, Adolphus. Read what you want.'

Upon hearing these words, Adolf knew that he'd found someone worthy of his friendship. He'd had many acquaintances in his life – Hanisch, whom he had met in the Asyl at Meidling, Josef Neumann the art dealer, a one-eyed locksmith named Robinson. From Neumann he had once accepted the gift of a frock-coat and a pair of woollen mittens only slightly darned across the knuckles. Hanisch had taught him how to survive the winters, shown him what buildings he might loiter in to avoid the cold, where to find free handouts of food, how to earn a few kreuzer shovelling coal or humping baggage at the station nearby. Hanisch had even taught him the words of 'Watch on the Rhine' one night when, both cold and hungry, they grew quite hysterical with misery and could have been mistaken for drunk. But in his heart he had never thought of either Neumann or Hanisch as his friends. It was true he'd become almost fond of Gustl, the young musician from Linz, but it hadn't lasted. First time round Gustl had passed the examination into the Academy of Music. With Meyer, Adolf sensed there would be no such betrayal. Meyer was old and could be trusted not to succeed where he himself had failed.

Taking seriously the invitation to visit the downstairs room whenever he wished, Adolf began to spend most evenings there, reading at the table until midnight. Sometimes Meyer, leaving the Adelphi by the side door, would find the young man waiting dog-like in the alley-way. Then, talking obsessively about various operatic productions he had seen in Vienna, Adolf would escort his friend home, never failing to remark that Meyer's nightly playing of great musical works was of supreme importance. 'You may be right,' Meyer would murmur, jaded from an evening's rendering of such classic pieces as the 'Cock-a-Doodle Rag' and 'Hitchy Koo' and 'Everybody's Doin' It Now'.

Alois grumbled frequently. Though he didn't particularly relish the company of his half-brother, he was annoyed at his behaviour. He said he was sick of Adolf treating the upstairs room as a hotel, coming in for meals and rushing out again.

'You presume too much,' he criticised. 'Meyer likes his privacy. It reflects badly on me.'

'I presume nothing,' cried Adolf, 'I understand him perfectly.'

Meyer gave him a top-coat which though warm was over-large. Bridget was always meaning to turn up the sleeves. It billowed about him as he walked. It had originally belonged, Meyer said, to a relation. Adolf thought the relation must have money to burn because the coat

66

was practically unworn. In the same wardrobe hung a jacket of dark blue with buttons of gold. Beneath it, placed neatly side by side and stuffed with paper, were a pair of golfing shoes. Secretly Adolf thought the jacket splendid and was disappointed he wasn't asked to try it on for size. Instead, Meyer foisted on him a pair of elastic-sided boots.

'I don't need boots,' Adolf protested. 'There's nothing wrong with the ones I'm wearing.'

He was mystified at Meyer's insistence. The boots, being of supple leather, took him by surprise – he bounced as he stepped. When Bridget finished the shirt she was making and showed it to him, he was genuinely delighted. He changed into it at once.

Alois, seeing him strutting about the front room, eyeing himself in the mirror above the fireplace, couldn't help smiling.

'It's a queer colour,' he said.

Adolf took no notice. The brown shirt meant he needn't sit wrapped in a blanket while his other one was in the wash. He hadn't been so well-dressed for years. Sometimes, if the wind was behind him, in his spring-heeled boots and his voluminous coat he flapped down the hill like a black crow. Meyer had to run to keep up with him.

Several mornings a week, whatever the weather, Meyer showed him something of the city. They would walk along

67

Huskisson Street past the five-storey houses, built for the shipping owners and the cotton brokers, pillars and steps of granite at the front entrance and stabling at the back for carriage horses: every house decaying now, the stables torn down, the windows smashed, each one inhabited by a dozen families or more, their washing hanging sodden on the wrought-iron balconies and a herd of ragged children squealing pig-like in the gutter.

'The rich have gone long since,' observed Meyer. 'Fled to the hills where the air is cleaner.'

'Clean air or not,' Adolf told him, 'I have never been so well.'

It was true. Even though the air was damp and in the past he'd been subject to bronchitis – here he felt exhilarated and full of energy. It had to do, he thought, with some quality of the northern light: the blackened city seemed to sail in an ocean of white sky, perpetually racing before the wind.

'You're just eating properly,' Meyer said. 'And then, of course, you don't work.'

On the corner of Hope Street, in a house with broken windows, lived Meyer's friend, Dr Kephalus. His door faced St James's cemetery. Whenever they drew close to the house Adolf quickened his pace or darted away over the road, pretending to be absorbed in a distant architectural detail. He didn't like sharing Meyer with anyone. Then Meyer, smiling to himself, followed patiently. They would stand at the railings looking down into the cemetery below or descending by the path, meander between laurel and dusty rhododendron, discussing the merits of the new cathedral, one third built, rising like an improbable airship out of the sunken graveyard. Last year it had been taller and the year before taller still.

'They keep knocking it down,' said Meyer, 'and starting all over again. Once it resembled a child's sandcastle. Whatever it is they're after, it seems to evade them.' Soon, he fancied, the structure might escape altogether; bursting from its moorings, it would lift, zeppelin-shaped and pink as a rose, into the scudding clouds.

Always Meyer took Adolf to the Pier Head. They stood, buffeted by wind, facing the mile-wide strip of river separating Liverpool from New Brighton. The ferry boats, encircled by screaming gulls, ploughed the muddy stretch of water towards the bulbous domes of the pleasure gardens and back again. Shouting to make himself heard, Meyer stabbed his finger at the skyline and named the docks, the Battery and the distant Welsh hills. He spoke of sailing ships forced to wait a dozen tides before floating into the Mersey, of the construction of the docks, of cholera, of how the monopolies of the great trading companies – the Hudson Bay, the Royal Africa, the East India – had eventually been broken. Finally, placing his arm enthusiastically about Adolf's shoulder he would swing him round and point at St Nicholas's church, the offices of the Docks and Harbour Board, and the vast bulk of the Royal Liver Building, its twin towers set with clocks like full moons and those giant birds, green wings spread, crouched under the sky. 'Consider,' he would bellow, 'the advantages of cast iron.'

His lectures, delivered in the teeth of the wind, entire sentences blown away, excited and silenced Adolf. Adolf didn't wish to appear stupid. He stood with his hands thrust deep into the pockets of his fluttering coat, an expression of eager concentration on his gaunt face. All he wanted, deep down, was for Meyer to compare him favourably with the buildings, the people, the past. At times like these Meyer considered him a good listener.

Shortly after midday, footsore and exhausted by the sound of his own voice, Meyer would suggest they go to the Kardomah Café or to a public house. Adolf invariably refused. 'Ah,' Meyer would exclaim. 'I had forgotten you were a lone wolf.' Thanking him profusely, Adolf would shake him by the hand and return to the house in Stanhope Street. He didn't want Meyer to tire of him, and besides he hadn't a halfpenny to his name. For an hour or so he'd help Bridget in small ways, carrying coals up from the cellar, rolling sheets of newspaper into wads to stuff along the cracks of the window frames. Remembering summer holidays in Spital when as a boy he had played near the blacksmith's forge, he began to hammer a length of steel-piping into the semblance of a handle. He would kneel at the grate, the metal red-hot from the fire, and tap away at it with the heavy end of the poker. Bridget was terrified he might burn a hole in the carpet. 'I know what I'm doing,' he assured her, thinking it was typical of Alois to have a gramophone and no means of winding it up.

Sometimes he would spend half an hour playing with the baby, tickling him under the chin or blowing gently into his face until the child blinked and gurgled and butted his forehead against the brown shirt. Then it was time to go downstairs and put the kettle on the stove in readiness for Meyer's return.

Adolf had now been residing in Liverpool for five weeks. It was difficult for him to remember that he had ever lived anywhere else, so secure did he feel, so cosily at home.

11

'How long are you staying?' asked Meyer, a week later. They were walking up the Boulevard towards the park.

Adolf stumbled and nearly fell. He had just finished discussing certain aspects of Alois's character – his greed, his stupidity, his tendency to boast. He had then referred briefly to the time Alois was sent to prison. After all, on that occasion Alois had been little more than a youth. No malice was intended. Meyer, with his seemingly innocent enquiry had rapped him over the knuckles as though he were a little boy who needed to be taught his manners. The bourgeois rebuke was obvious – he shouldn't bite the hand that fed him. Surely it went without saying that Alois provided him with food and lodging? Did Meyer take him for a fool? Had he not been so deeply wounded he might have borrowed Alois's phrase and shouted in Meyer's face that it took two to make the bargain. It was the word 'staying' that hurt most, implying that there was somewhere

72

else he belonged. Dear God, he had been so confident of Meyer's ability to understand him that he could have wept.

'I am fifty-four,' announced Meyer, continuing to pace the gravel walk as though nothing had happened. 'I came here when I was twenty. I left Berlin thinking I would be absent for a few weeks. I did not mean to stay.'

'I have no intention of staying,' cried Adolf instantly. He was so distressed he lost his sense of direction and began to bump into trees.

'Mrs O'Leary is a different case,' Meyer said. 'She came here when she was a small child. In a sense she is not a foreigner. I have never been anything else. If you can believe the newspapers, myself and others like me are the sole cause of all the trouble in this town. We have infiltrated the Corn Exchange, the shops, the restaurants, the theatre orchestras. The agitators complain that we take employment away from the decent English working man. And have you any idea who he is, my young friend? Why, he is an Irishman.'

He glanced curiously at Adolf who, with clenched fists, was veering from side to side on the path.

'Let us sit down,' Meyer suggested. 'I am out of breath.'

They sat at some distance from one another on a bench under a tree. They were sandwiched between two roads along which the trams rattled in either direction. The rain fell steadily, dripping from branch to branch, forming puddles in the hollows of the path.

'A decade before I arrived,' Meyer said, 'water was supplied to the houses on only three mornings a week. Even for the rich. Just think of it.'

It was difficult to tell whether Adolf was thinking of it or not; he was staring morosely at the toe-caps of his muddy boots.

'First I was in Munich,' Meyer reminisced. 'Then Berlin. In neither place did it rain so often as here.'

Still Adolf made no response.

Meyer searched his mind for a topic of conversation that would raise the young man's spirits. For some reason Adolf seemed to have fallen into an abrupt and black depression. His face was quite contorted with misery.

'You would like Munich,' Meyer remarked. 'It is a city of artists. It's not as beautiful as Vienna, but the people are more friendly.'

'Doubtless it's swarming with Jews,' Adolf said.

'German Jews, certainly,' agreed Meyer.

'It is my belief,' Adolf told him, in a voice querulous with despair, 'that European history is merely the history of racial struggle. The decline of the Roman Empire is a classic example of historical decadence resulting from contaminated blood. Like Rome, Europe is sinking under the burden of bastard peoples. Animals stick to their own kind. The tiger doesn't mate with the elephant.'

'It might prove difficult,' said Meyer. 'Unless the elephant could be persuaded to lose weight.'

'Impure blood,' shouted Adolf, 'spawns impure ideas and creeds. We've not only the Jews to contend with but the Slavs, the Socialists, the Hapsburg Monarchists, the Roman Catholics, the Croats . . .'

'There would seem to be no one left,' Meyer observed mildly.

'Europe is rotten at the core,' spluttered Adolf. 'Rotten.' He couldn't repeat the word often enough. That small adjective contained all the wretchedness he felt at Meyer's rejection of him. Let Meyer buy him a ticket tomorrow, to Munich, to Africa for all the difference it would make. School had been rotten, and his father, and Linz and Vienna. Even his beloved mother had died rotten of a cancer. It was a rotten world.

'My dear boy,' said Meyer kindly, concerned by the whiteness of his face. 'You are too sensitive. You shouldn't upset yourself so much.' He tried to pat Adolf's arm, but the young man shrugged him off. 'It will be no comfort to you,' Meyer said, 'but we have all felt the same at your age. Over one obsession or another. With me it was music. I wanted to be a success. I dreamed of being famous.'

'Such things don't interest me,' muttered Adolf, lying.

He was behaving, Meyer thought, for all the world as though they'd had a lovers' tiff. 'I'm going to visit my friend Kephalus,' he said firmly. 'You should come too. He is a remarkable man, a man of the world. He will cheer you up.' He stood and waited a moment.

Adolf couldn't resist one last parting shot. 'If Alois is doing so well in business,' he said, 'why on earth does he play the waiter at night?'

'A man,' replied Meyer quietly, 'needs capital. So they tell me.'

He began to walk briskly away down the avenue of trees. He half expected Adolf to remain where he was or to disappear in the opposite direction. However, when he reached the dairy and looked back before crossing Upper Parliament Street Adolf was behind him, sullen, but following.

12

Partly Adolf was curious to meet Dr Kephalus. He had heard Alois refer to him as a maniac. If Alois's sense of judgment ran true to form then undoubtedly the doctor would prove to be exceptionally sane and composed. He was beginning also to feel that he had reacted foolishly to Meyer's question. When Meyer asked him how long he intended to stay in Liverpool he had possibly meant that he hoped it was for a long time. Probably he had been about to suggest alternative accommodation, away from Alois and his constantly belittling remarks. Bridget had told him that the rooms on the third floor were unoccupied. There was an attic too, rented by a commercial traveller who was never there.

Kephalus himself opened the door of the house with broken windows. He was holding to his lips a cigarette plunged in a long ivory tube and blowing smoke-rings. His eyes were so large and discoloured, like those of an old sick horse left out in a field, that Adolf was startled. He took a step backwards and was nudged forward again by Meyer. Between leaving the hall and entering the back room, Meyer aged twenty years. He became unctuous and sentimental and began rubbing his hands together as if he were cold.

'At last,' he pronounced, 'my two friends are facing one another.'

It wasn't strictly true. Kephalus was six-foot tall and looking down on Adolf, who shrank both from the gaze of those rainbow-tinted eyes and from the overpowering smell of perspiration and tobacco that pervaded the doctor's clothing.

'Sit down, sit down,' commanded Kephalus, pushing Adolf towards a solitary chair beside a little round table at the window. Apart from a bookcase and an upturned crate near the hearth, the room was bare of furniture. Above the fireplace, festooned with cobwebs, jutted the head of an antelope with spiralled horns.

'So you are the artist?' said Kephalus, towering over Adolf in his rickety chair.

'No,' he said, 'I am no longer an artist.'

'Then you are a student, perhaps?' The doctor spoke German fluently but with a strange, harsh accent.

'Yes,' said Adolf reluctantly.

'A student of what, may I ask?'

'At the moment,' Adolf said stiffly, 'I have not decided.'

'An undecided student,' cried Kephalus boisterously, and he clapped Adolf so heartily on the shoulder that he was in danger of falling off his chair.

Having discomfited him by such questions, the doctor proceeded to ignore him. There being nothing to sit on, he and Meyer began to pace the floor, talking volubly, the one still rubbing his hands gleefully together, the other gesturing wildly and lighting one cigarette after another. Kephalus was wearing a grey shirt and a black silk tie under a crumpled jacket; as he moved, quantities of ash spilled from him. Now and then he leaned against the wall in real or mock despair and covered his alarming face with the crook of his arm. His hands, Adolf noticed, were those of a labourer, thick and swollen, with nails so deformed and shortened that it seemed he must at one time have trapped his fingers in a door. The two men were talking about some incident of violence that had taken place two days previously.

'The shame of it,' cried Kephalus at one point. 'The shame of it.'

'Next time,' Meyer said, 'we will be better prepared.'

Kephalus then launched into a description of the injuries received by certain persons. 'The fellow who was heckling us earlier in the evening,' he said, 'the one with the squint – had a broken jaw and contusions to the left side of his face. I put twelve stitches into Michael Murphy's scalp. The Connolly woman has internal bleeding from

79

a boot in her belly. She's in the Infirmary now. That child in Maguire Street had his foot crushed, but it was an accident.'

'And Constable Rafferty?' asked Meyer.

'Dead,' said Kephalus. 'I thought you were told. He broke his neck when they shoved him off the roof.'

What in God's name, fretted Adolf, did Meyer see in the dreadful doctor, standing there rolling his baleful, stallion eyes and waving his arms like a madman as he spat from beneath those nicotine-stained moustaches the most revolting details of his trade? Kephalus, he understood, was attached to the local police division and attended only those cases that came under their auspices. If there was a fire involving loss of life at a warehouse or a fatality on the docks, an explosion in the engine room, a suicide or some poor brute mangled in the machinery of the saw mills, they sent for him. By the sound of it he was more undertaker than healer. Adolf would have been morbidly interested in the conversation but for the fact that he was excluded from it.

Just then the doctor, who was in the middle of a particularly lurid account of a scalded stoker whose skin had peeled away from his body in layers like an over-ripe onion, turned to him and said: 'I believe there is a difficulty concerning your papers. They are made out in the wrong name. We will have to find you new ones.'

Before Adolf could confirm or deny that he had any

such problem he was asked if he would take a glass of wine.

He was on the point of accepting when Meyer said: 'He doesn't drink, but like you he has a sweet tooth. One of your sugary cakes would be most appreciated.'

'Excellent,' cried Kephalus, and he bounded from the room, trailing smoke.

'A remarkable man,' burst out Meyer, 'isn't he?'

'Very,' said Adolf.

'Do not,' warned Meyer, 'talk to him of racial struggles or contaminated blood. He is not as tolerant as I am, nor as small. He has a fist like a sledge-hammer.'

Adolf made no reply. On one occasion when living at the Männerheim he had become involved in a political discussion with two transport workers. They were sitting in the cellar kitchen, having just finished their evening meal, and he was preparing his at the stove. During the ensuing argument – left versus right, Darwinism, the unification of Germany – it emerged that his two opponents belonged to a labour organisation formed by the Social Democrats. He had promptly called them lunatics. Rising united from the table they flung his fried egg into the banked-up snow outside the window and thumped him mercilessly. He was left lying on the greasy floor with his lip split and his nose bleeding. He had still managed, through a bubble of blood, to repeat that they were lunatics. Did Meyer imagine he couldn't take care of himself?

He stared impassively out of the window at a yard only slightly less dingy than the room he was occupying. He began to wonder if perhaps Meyer wasn't deeply frivolous. How else could he tolerate such totally unrewarding characters as Mary O'Leary and Alois and the unspeakable Dr Kephalus? Every evening he met Alois and had a drink with him, including those nights they were both employed in the same hotel. On Sundays, after eating his dinner in her company Meyer promenaded along the Boulevard with the hairy Mary O'Leary or took a ride on the ferry with her to Seacombe. He didn't seem to notice her tatty bonnet or those men's boots she wore under her torn and wretched petticoats. He never alluded to her moustache. And now it was painfully obvious that Meyer actually preferred to talk of first-degree burns or the effect on a human body of a ton of grain dropped from a height, rather than ponder the more subtle impression made by art and philosophy and music. He too was a lunatic.

Kephalus returned and set down on the table a chipped plate on which wobbled three custard tarts.

'How kind,' murmured Meyer, seeing that Adolf's mouth was clamped tight. The doctor went to the bookcase and took from the top shelf a half-empty bottle and two glasses.

'My mother,' said Adolf, 'died of cancer. She was treated with iodoform. At the end she couldn't swallow.'

'Iodoform,' Kephalus told him, 'has fallen into disrepute. At the time it was one of the wonders of medicine. Unfortunately it had such side effects as you mention.'

Adolf was scandalised at this casual admission of malpractice. He was more than ever convinced that physicians were an ignorant aristocracy kept afloat by witchcraft and the pathetic need of relations to witness miracles. 'She thought it was helping her,' he said accusingly.

'Well then,' reasoned Kephalus, 'it probably did. I well remember attending a man on the deck of a ship who had been eating a hunk of bread when a hawser snapped. It sliced through him like a wire through cheese. He was severed practically in half. With his dying breath he asked me to give him something to make him better. In the circumstances a pellet of bread was as good as anything else. He expired thirty seconds later with a look of unutterable relief in his eyes. Eat your cake.'

Adolf stared at the creamy surface of the custard tart dusted with cinnamon and saw the speckled skin of his mother's constricted throat. He feared he was going to be sick.

'Death is everywhere,' said Kephalus. 'We are essentially fragile. We don't have to wait for the sword or some other equally sensational weapon to strike us down. One may go just as easily with the measles or diphtheria, meningitis, colic, influenza or mere hunger. There are so many ways of dying it's astonishing any of us choose old age.'

'May I open the window?' interrupted Adolf.

He was told it was impossible, the sash-cords having long since rotted away.

'None of us,' continued the doctor, loping about the room in his great dusty boots, 'fully appreciates how easily we can be snuffed out. In my work I see such things that would make us live each day as though it were the last.'

'True, true,' agreed Meyer. Cheerfully he raised his glass and drank.

'Imagine,' proposed the doctor, fixing Adolf with his terrible eyes, 'a young girl from Scotland and a big buck nigger from the Cameroons.' He approached the table and locked his stubby thumbs together an inch from Adolf's face. 'It's a dark night and she's teetering along a little the worse for drink beneath the arches of the Overhead Railway. She's humming to herself. For once she's got a few coppers in her purse and a bed to go to. She doesn't see him because he's the Prince of Darkness, but he sees her.'

He paused. Meyer's breathing was audible.

Suddenly the doctor shouted: 'Straight up her nostrils!' And making a noise with his mouth like a piece of silk being ripped asunder he wrenched his thumbs apart.

Having removed the stud from the collar of Adolf's brown shirt, Kephalus picked him up bodily and carried him down the hall. He opened the front door and sat him on the top step. A dog ran from across the road and trotted backwards and forwards on the pavement, sniffing. 'You don't breathe properly,' Kephalus said, and he forced Adolf's head down between his knees and held it there with one finger while he blew a cloud of smoke at the dog.

13

At first Alois didn't notice that Adolf had taken to the couch again. He thought he was sleeping late and retiring early. He discovered the truth when he returned in the middle of the day to collect some samples he needed. Bridget was at the table giving the baby his dinner. He asked her if Adolf was ill.

'No,' she said. 'I'm sure he's not ill.'

'Is he eating?'

'Like a horse,' she said. It was only because she cooked him food all the time. Actually, she felt Adolf would be quite happy subsisting on a diet of jam butties.

'How long has he been like this?'

'Three days,' she replied truthfully. She understood his point of view. It wasn't fair Adolf lying in state, living off the fat of the land, so to speak, while Alois spent his waking hours wearing out his shoe leather in an attempt to better himself.

Gripping the sleeper roughly by the shoulder, Alois rolled him off the couch and on to the floor. 'I'm not angry,' he shouted, the little veins purple in his cheeks. 'I've no objection to a man lounging about till Kingdom Come if he pleases, so long as it's in his own house and at his own expense. You can pack your bags and go.'

'Go,' said Adolf. 'Go where?'

'What the hell is it to me,' fumed Alois. 'Back where you came from. Anywhere you like. You didn't care where I was going all those years ago.'

Adolf made no attempt to rise from his knees. He crouched there clasping and unclasping his hands like a penitent schoolboy. In the time between dreams and hitting the floor his face had lost its look of stupor and acquired a haunted expression.

'You're welcome to the blankets,' cried Alois, picking them off the carpet and throwing them at him. He strode to the hearth and seized hold of the length of bent piping. 'And you can take this bloody work of art with you.'

He hurled the metal with all his strength towards the couch. It skimmed the air a fraction above Adolf's head and struck the wall. Rebounding, it clattered harmlessly to the floor. Alois ran into the adjoining room and slammed the door behind him. The baby, chuckling, waved its fists.

'He might have brained you,' said Bridget, looking severely at Adolf. She left darling Pat in his chair and followed her husband into the bedroom.

'God forgive me,' whispered Alois. 'I could have been up on a murder charge.'

'You missed,' she consoled him. 'He'd try the patience of a saint.'

'Once,' he said, 'when I needed real help he wrote and told me to go hang myself.'

'He never,' she cried. 'You shouldn't give him house room.'

'It was signed in my stepmother's name,' he said. 'But it was in his handwriting.'

She couldn't think how to comfort him. They had grown so far apart. She was ashamed of herself for feeling a little glow of pleasure at his misery.

'I don't know what to do for the best,' Alois said forlornly. He was used to making iron decisions. There was nowhere Adolf could go. He hadn't the price of a tram ticket. He prowled back and forth between the bed and the wardrobe.

'Take off your hat,' said Bridget. 'You're sweating cobs.' She fetched a towel from the back of a chair and watched while he mopped his perspiring face.

'Am I being unreasonable, Bridie?' he asked.

She grew flustered. He hadn't called her by that name or sought her advice for a long time.

She said loyally: 'No, you're not. You're in the right of it entirely. He can't live the rest of his life horizontal in our front room. He should go home or find himself employment.'

'He hasn't a home to go to. He's blotted his copybook. Angela won't have him.'

'The cheek of him,' she cried. 'Loafing around . . . sponging off you.'

'Ah, well,' said Alois. 'We can't all be breadwinners. It's not his fault if he hasn't found what he's good at. He was always jumping from one thing to another . . . drawing, reading, studying maps. When he wasn't doing that he was playing cowboys and Indians. Why, on the day of his confirmation he came back from the cathedral and without bothering to change his clothes he was off with his friends and he didn't come home until nightfall. Aunt Johanna had come and my cousins. We never saw him, but you could hear him for miles around, whooping.'

'Whooping!' said Bridget.

'On the war-path in the orchard.'

'On such a day,' said Bridget, shocked. Suddenly she saw that Alois was smiling, standing there with his hat pushed to the back of his head and the towel still in his hand. 'What's up with you?' she asked.

'Did you hear me telling him to pack his bags? If he had any, he wouldn't have anything to put in them.'

Bridget refused to see the humour in it. People had no business travelling the world unequipped. Though she'd been relieved to see the back of Adolf when first he had gone out every day, she was riddled with envy for the company he kept. She hadn't set eyes on Meyer for weeks. Her apparent hostility towards the young man had a contrary effect on Alois. A moment ago he'd been prepared to tip Adolf down the stairs. Now he perched himself on the side of the bed and thought carefully what he should do. He could of course use some of his hard-earned savings and buy Adolf a return ticket to Vienna, but that was doing no more than sweeping the problem under the carpet. Adolf had already squandered a fortune. To pretend that he'd ever been a penniless student was sheer humbug. At one time his income must have amounted to fifty crowns a month, what with the inheritance from his father and his mother's legacy, not to mention the considerable sum left to him by his aunt, Johanna Polzl. No sacrifice was involved when he relinquished his orphan's pension in favour of Angela. God knows where the money had gone. He wasn't a drinking man or a gambler, nor did he seem to bother with women. By the cut of him he certainly hadn't spent any of it on clothes. Definitely Adolf needed guidance. It shouldn't prove too difficult to handle him – though prone to tantrums he was easily intimidated. He was also lazy, self-opinionated, and unlikely to win prizes for his sense of humour. Only the other week while eating a hearty supper he announced he'd starve in the gutter rather than join in the stampede for wealth and power. No doubt about it, washing a few dishes would do him the world of good. He stood, his mind made up, and told Bridget: 'I shall try to get him a position at the Adelphi. It's nearly Christmas and with the banquets and parties they'll need extra labour in the kitchens.'

'Sweet Jesus,' exclaimed Bridget, appalled. 'You'll lose your place for recommending the likes of him.'

'Nonsense,' he said. 'Stay here while I have a private word.'

Adolf was sitting dejectedly on the couch, clutching his blankets. He and darling Pat were eyeing one another unhappily across the carpet, each convinced that they had been left alone for ever.

Alois sat too. 'It's not good for a young man to do nothing,' he began. 'The mind goes dull. A man needs to work.'

'I read,' protested Adolf. 'I read all the time.'

'Reading is a luxury,' said Alois, determined at all costs to remain calm. 'You don't see *me* with my nose in a book. Life is more than a game. It isn't all cowboys and Indians. A man has responsibilities.'

Adolf made no reply. Obviously, he thought, Alois had never forgotten the time he had been struck in the calf by a wooden arrow aimed from the cemetery wall. He hadn't even bled.

'One needs,' said Alois, 'to go out into the streets and earn a living. You can't remain in the paddock for ever. In the parlance of the race course, you should test yourself over the flat. One must gain form.' He paused and looked sharply at his brother who, with eyes half-closed and a vacant expression on his face, appeared about to fall sideways on to the cushions. 'You seem to require an inordinate amount of sleep,' he remarked as mildly as he was able. 'In my opinion it's due to lack of fresh air and stimulation, but perhaps there's a medical explanation. Possibly we should let Dr Kephalus examine you.'

'That man!' said Adolf, roused. 'He'd be better employed in a butcher's shop.'

'There I sympathise with you,' agreed Alois. 'It's difficult to think of the exact word to describe him.'

'"Disgusting" springs readily to mind,' said Adolf. He was now wide-awake and prepared to discuss Dr Kephalus at length.

Alois cut him short. If Meyer considered the doctor brilliant and dedicated – why, then he must be. What Adolf thought was of little importance. 'I myself,' he said righteously, 'have learnt to keep my own council. Things go on here that I don't approve of, but I neither interfere nor criticise.'

'What things?' asked Adolf.

'I've my livelihood to think of,' replied Alois cryptically. 'Besides, it's not my house.'

'Kephalus offered to supply me with certain documents,' said Adolf.

At this Alois abruptly stood and held up his hand for silence. 'Say no more,' he ordered. 'I refuse to be involved. It's none of my business.'

'Someone,' insinuated Adolf, 'was involved in the first place. I never mentioned my papers.' He thought his brother ridiculous, standing there with one arm raised as though halting the traffic, his face turned to the baby who, bored and fretful, was uttering querulous little cries like a hen scratching in a yard.

'Now look here,' shouted Alois, adopting a bullying tone. 'There's something we must resolve here and now. I simply can't go on supporting you. It's not as if you're crippled or have a weak heart. We haven't met in fifteen years. Why should I put food in your mouth?'

'Why indeed,' murmured Adolf sarcastically. The way Alois expressed it he might have been a fledgling in a nest, beak constantly open for worms. He knew he was in the wrong. He tried to assume an attitude of contrition, of self-abasement. Nothing happened. He continued to feel contempt for his expensively clothed brother. 'I expect,' he couldn't resist saying, 'it's on account of your superior and unselfish nature.'

Alois, infuriated, was on the point of frog-marching him down the stairs and booting him out of the door when he suddenly noticed the section of twisted metal up-ended against the skirting board. Sobered, he made one last effort. Taking care to avoid darling Pat's sticky and outstretched hands, he began to walk round and round the table. 'I'll make myself plain,' he announced firmly. 'You can't stay here any longer. Not unless you're willing to work. That's my final word.'

Instantly Adolf was alarmed. This time he was convinced his brother was serious. He was certain he would never survive another winter in Vienna – destitute, the authorities searching for him. 'I'm not afraid to work,' he cried. 'I've shovelled snow before now. I've shovelled till the skin swelled up in blisters.'

'There's not much call for that here,' said Alois. 'Mostly it rains. I had something less strenuous in mind. And in beautiful surroundings. As an artist you know better than I how important such things are. You couldn't fail to be impressed . . . such ceilings . . . such decor . . . the most sumptuous rooms imaginable.' He was carried away by his own eloquence. As he spoke he trailed his fingers expressively in the air, conjuring marvels. The child at the table followed the movements of his father's hand and, mistaking the ring he wore for a bright toy, wriggled frantically in his chair. 'You have never seen such statues . . . Each article of furniture is exquisitely carved . . . The curtains are magnificent. You'll be serving people of refinement and learning, rubbing shoulders with the highest in the land. You will swoon at the exchange of ideas. Believe me, it will come as a revelation to you – the main carpet alone is worth a thousand pounds.' Alois was standing stock-still now, one hand upraised above the whiteness of his cuff. He appeared to hold his brother's future between thumb and forefinger like a rose.

'Serving!' said Adolf.

'It's not all that definite,' Alois said hastily. 'I may not be able to swing it. I can but try. I suggest you meet me outside the Adelphi at six this evening. The front entrance. Be sure to polish your boots and wear the white shirt.' Relieved that he had managed to refrain from violence, he added generously: 'As a gambling man I'd put my money on you every time. You're a winner if ever I saw one. You have so many advantages – youth, an excellent brain, a good background—'

'Background,' repeated Adolf.

'Decent parents, a stable home. As a man grows older he realises these things.' Alois glanced sentimentally in the direction of old man Hitler and bowed his head.

Outraged by this lamentable distortion of the truth, Adolf jumped to his feet.

'Decent?' he bellowed. 'He was illegitimate and so were you. He married three blasted times. You were beaten so regularly that if you dropped those elegant trousers we'd still see the marks of his belt.'

'It takes two to make the bargain,' muttered Alois. 'One adjusts, one appreciates—'

'One bloody doesn't,' cried Adolf. 'He was a bastard. Both of you. Bastards.' And gibbering with loathing he ran to the hat-stand and leaping in the air spat a gob of saliva at the photograph on the wall.

The baby, startled, arched its back and screamed.

14

Yet at precisely six o'clock Adolf was waiting outside the Adelphi Hotel. His white shirt had proved unwearable; the collar was frayed beyond repair. Reluctantly Bridget had lent him a tray-cloth embroidered at the edges with bunches of cherries, which in some fashion he had stuffed inside the revers of his black coat. He waited for what seemed like a long time, holding a newspaper over his head to protect himself from the rain. Several times he started to climb the steps towards the commissionaire who guarded the entrance to the building, and on each occasion he lost courage half-way up and turned back. He wouldn't risk a rebuff. He constantly rearranged the white cloth more securely inside his coat, fumbling there in the drizzle like a woman adjusting a troublesome shoulder strap. Below him in the main thoroughfare the pedestrians swarmed amid the tram-cars and the bicycles; they surged backwards and forwards across the street, intent on appointments and destinations. Everyone, it seemed, save him, had some place to go, some function to perform. The ramp on which he stood was flooded with light. Along the entire length of the hotel dark figures were silhouetted against the brightness, seated at tables, standing, gesticulating; floor after floor of blazing windows rose into the night. When taxi-cabs approached the kerb, the commissionaire hurtled down the steps holding aloft a large brown umbrella. As the cabs rolled to a halt he tugged open the doors and the occupants ducked into the light. Between one dry interior and another the women hovered for a moment, jostling for space and hoisting their skirts above the wet paving stones. Then Adolf scurried out of their way, fearful of being ordered to move on, his head bent underneath the piece of sodden newspaper. It was torture to him. As the women pranced upwards under the bobbing umbrella, he distinctly heard them sniggering. He watched like a beggar as the gentlemen followed more leisurely and entered the revolving doors. Laughter spilled down the steps as they spun round into the glittering foyer. All that remained of their giddy ascent of wealth and privilege was a faint aroma of perfume and cigars.

Thinking perhaps that he had misunderstood his brother's instructions, Adolf trailed up the alleyway and loitered outside the tradesmen's entrance. From inside came a continuous din of banging doors and voices raised.

Round his feet cats circled, waiting for food. Throwing away his newspaper he sat on a dustbin for half an hour. He remembered Meyer telling him that the site on which the hotel was built had once been a place for picnicking. It amused him, perched on his bin, overshadowed by cast iron and bricks, the stench of decaying food in his nostrils and a gush of greasy water from kitchens and laundry constantly flooding into the gutter, to think that he sat in a strawberry field. It was only when he looked upwards to where the stars should have been that he felt depressed and out of sorts. At last, abandoning all hope of meeting Alois, he stood, shook himself like a dog and descending the hill again turned into Lime Street.

He wasn't too disturbed. After all he couldn't be blamed. He had arrived in the right place at the right time. Bridget would vouch for him. She had been annoyed, to say the least, by his gesture of defiance towards old man Hitler. 'You'd think it was cuckoo time,' was all she'd said; but those rosy patches had ebbed from her cheeks when she wiped the spittle from the hat-stand. She was however a Catholic and frightened of irritating God. She'd have to tell the truth, and she'd have to be believed. Why else would he have borrowed that ridiculous bib and spent an hour buffing the leather of his boots with a scrap of silk petticoat? He wasn't sure why Alois had failed to show up. Doubtless at this moment he was propping up some bar, talking of razor blades.

When Adolf crossed the road and began to walk down Church Street he was revolted to see that the shop windows were filled with seasonal displays. The dummies in fur coats sat on sledges festooned with sprigs of holly and piled high with scarlet-ribboned packages. St Nicholas, a sack on his shoulder, stood in a meadow of cottonwool sprinkled with mica. Above the scarves and the handkerchieves and the blouses with the Peter Pan collars hung glass baubles and paper lanterns. He found such sights detestable. The night his mother died he had run to fetch Dr Bloch, and on their return, thrusting open the door, the candles had wavered in the draught. In his mother's eyes he saw reflected those tiny flickering lights. When she was dead Dr Bloch had closed her lids with two deft dabs of his thumb. The candles on the tree burned on.

Nauseated by the appearance of a stuffed robin in the window of a jeweller's shop, perched on a papier mâché log with a loop of pearls dangling from its beak, Adolf recrossed the road to Clayton Square. Despite the rain the old women draped in shawls were selling fruit, though for some reason they had abandoned their usual pitch on the pavement and now stood well back against the facade of the restaurant. Naphtha flares set in buckets were spaced at intervals along the cobblestones, and a policeman, holding a lantern, patrolled up and down. Avoiding him, Adolf made a small detour round the square and hovered outside the picture house, peering in through the doors at the signed photographs of glamorous actresses, faces posed peek-a-boo over milk-white shoulders or haughtily smiling with black lips curved above a mist of furs. He couldn't afford to go inside and he couldn't go home. Not yet. At this hour Bridget would be crooning her Irish lullabys as she sponged the baby in front of the fire.

Regretfully he turned away from the lighted doors and walked across the cobblestones towards the main street. He fell full-length over the trunk of a giant tree that was lying on the ground, its branches tied with cord. For a moment he lay there believing himself to have been miraculously transported to the pine forests of Leonding.

He was plucked upright by the policeman, who demanded to know if he was blind as well as clumsy. A small crowd had lined up in the square, separated from the winded Adolf by the barrier of the furled Christmas tree. He put his left foot to the ground and winced. Among the interested spectators stood a young woman with a painted face and a whalebone comb stuck in her wet hair. Clambering over the obstruction she poked Adolf's lacerated chin with her finger and told him he was bleeding.

'Thank you, thank you,' he muttered, horribly embarrassed. He was convinced she was a prostitute.

'What do you think those are for?' asked the policeman,

indicating the row of buckets lit with flames. He held his lantern higher and scrutinised the tree for damage. 'It's Corporation property,' he warned.

'Bugger the corporation,' cried the young woman. 'Can't you see he's hurt hisself?' Protectively she put one arm round Adolf and began to push him further on down the street.

Desperately he glanced back and seeing a face he instantly recognised shouted: 'Please, I need assistance.'

The man he so imploringly addressed stared at him, hesitated, and vaulted agilely across the tree. Catching up with them, he spoke to the girl. She frowned, her hand resting on Adolf's waist.

'Be off with you,' ordered the man.

At this the girl, glancing uneasily in the direction of the policeman, relinquished her hold and walked sulkily away. It was then that Adolf realised that he didn't know the bearded man after all. Conscious of some monstrous error, he gazed bewildered into the stranger's blue eyes and gritting his teeth manufully hobbled off down the street with as much speed as he could muster.

Not until he was approaching Hope Street did he slacken his pace. How, he wondered, had he made such a bloomer? The man hadn't known him from Adam. Possibly it had been a trick of the firelight – and yet . . . and yet . . . he could have sworn it was a face he knew. Mortified, he limped beside the railings of the cemetery, praying he wouldn't meet. Dr Kephalus. Thank God his ankle wasn't badly sprained. Already he felt less pain. It was a mercy, he thought, that he hadn't broken his leg. Alois, being a racing man, would probably have considered it kinder to shoot him.

He had decided when he reached the house to sneak into Meyer's room and bathe his foot. He could rest there until Bridget had gone to bed. But when he let himself into the hall, the door to the fiddler's room was open. He caught a glimpse of Mary O'Leary's backside as he crept like a thief up the stairs. What a dilemma! He was anxious to avoid Bridget – some time during his upsetting evening he had unaccountably mislaid the tray cloth embroidered with cherries. He wouldn't be at all surprised if the obliging prostitute hadn't whipped it from his breast when she first accosted him. Leaning against the banisters he removed his boots and carrying them in his arms stealthily passed the second landing and continued upwards.

It was pitch dark on the third floor. He tapped blindly along the passageway, groping for doors. One was padlocked, and the second, though not bolted in any way, refused to budge. He was frightened of putting his shoulder to the panelling in case he made a noise. With the third and final door at the extreme end of the corridor he struck lucky. It opened without a sound. Ahead of him he saw the dull gleam of window panes. Cautiously he closed the door behind him and limped forwards. He was looking down into the dance half across the street. For a time he watched the couples bounding and cavorting under the crimson streamers. He caught himself smiling with second-hand enjoyment. Sheepishly he glanced away and saw in the street below, leaning against the railings of a house, the solitary figure of a man with his arms crossed upon his chest. He appeared to be staring steadfastly at the shuttered windows of Meyer's room. Though it was too dark to see his features, Adolf knew immediately who he was. I'm afraid, he thought, and he ducked down out of sight, his knees trembling beneath him. For several weeks he had pushed from his mind his encounter with the mysterious stranger on the boat and the apparition of the bearded man on his balcony above the river. Now the nightmare was upon him again. He began to crawl on all fours towards the door. The pressure of the darkness seemed to advance like a tidal wave – he felt he was being pushed backwards. As he scuttled feebly over the rough floorboards a fearful racket broke out in the house next door. First there was a tremendous banging from below and then muffled footsteps pounding along passageways. Panic-stricken, Adolf clawed his way up the wall. He couldn't find the door knob; his fingers clutched something small and metallic, and the next instant electric light flooded the room. He spun round, mouth wide with shock.

The only furniture was a mattress on the floor, piled with rolls of paper. Above the window and along the length of the right-hand wall the plaster was peeling and ringed with patches of damp. Clearly the room was in the process of redecoration, for the wall to Adolf's left, from skirting board to picture rail, was covered in immaculately stretched paper. He slid downwards on to his haunches and stared in puzzlement at the pattern of full-blown roses on a cream ground. Was it possible that Meyer had secretly been preparing this room for him all along? It was the only logical explanation when he considered Meyer's deliberate questioning of him as to the length of his stay. Forgetting the sinister loiterer in the street below, Adolf crouched dreamily against the door, building shelves in his mind and stacking them with books. He didn't care for roses, but none the less . . .

Without warning a section of the newly decorated wall collapsed inwards and, as if fired through a paper hoop, a man with a bandage about his temples shot into the room. Lifting Adolf by the lapels of his coat he flung him aside and was out of the door and running down the stairs in a matter of seconds. Adolf was left in a heap on the floor, facing a jagged black hole in the wall, its edges scalloped with loops of torn paper printed with flowers. A fine drift of white dust began to settle on him. For a moment he lay there stunned, astonished that no sound had escaped his lips. Then he heard shouts coming from somewhere beyond the break in the wall. Scrambling to his feet, he had the presence of mind to switch off the light before fleeing down the passage.

15

He could get no sense out of either Bridget or Mary O'Leary, both of whom happened to be on the second-floor landing when he came barefooted down the stairs. They professed to have heard nothing out of the ordinary. Adolf pushed past them and looked excitedly about the sitting room.

'He had a bandage on his head,' he shouted. 'His shirt was unbuttoned at the front.' He tore open his coat and thumped his breast. 'I saw clearly a triangle of hair, just here.'

'Where's my tray cloth?' asked Bridget. Neither woman could understand what he was blabbering about.

'Aren't you ashamed?' admonished Mary O'Leary, gazing flabbergasted at his bare feet and naked chest. In vain Adolf tried to tell her about the noise, the running footsteps and the sudden disintegration of the solid and freshly papered wall. He said the man must still be in the house, hiding somewhere. The sounds from next door had been like an army of men on the rampage. They were probably creeping down the stairs towards them at this very moment, or possibly they were outside, surrounding the house. He shut the sitting-room door and wedged the back of a chair under the handle.

'Don't do that to my good chair,' scolded Bridget, and she put it back in its place at the table.

Striding to the window Mary O'Leary inspected the street below. 'An army!' she scoffed. 'Then they have dug themselves into trenches. There's no one out there.'

Adolf waited for Alois to come home. The two women warmed themselves at the fire and dug each other in the ribs from time to time.

'There's no mistake,' whispered Mary O'Leary. 'He's not all there.'

Alois returned in a cheerful state; something had gone well for him. He took from the pocket of his coat a chocolate soldier wrapped in silver paper and placed it on the table for the baby to find in the morning. He listened with a fatuous smile on his face to Bridget's tale. Eyeing the scratches on his brother's chin, he asked hopefully: 'Have you been drinking?' It occurred to him that Adolf might have given up his namby-pamby ways and become involved in a brawl.

'I was hardly in a position to drink,' snapped Adolf. 'I

spent the best part of two hours standing in the rain outside the Adelphi Hotel.'

'Ah, well,' Alois told him. 'There seemed no point. They haven't an opening for you until after Christmas.'

'Upstairs,' said Adolf. 'The wall fell in. I swear it. Come with me and look.' He jumped to his feet and caught hold of his brother's arm.

But Alois wouldn't budge. He said it was none of his business if the roof blew off.

Adolf's sleep was filled with nightmares. He dreamt his father held his mother by a hank of her long brown hair – with the open palm of his hand old man Hitler struck alternately her plump shoulders and those tear-stained wobbling cheeks. Adolf started up from the cushions convinced he heard the slap of flesh on flesh in the stillness of the night.

In the morning, before anyone in the house was awake, he left his couch and mounted the stairs.

The door on the third floor was ajar. From the end of the passage Adolf could see his boots placed neatly side by side on the mattress. When he entered the room he found there wasn't a particle of dust on the rough flooring. Someone had rubbed the toecaps of his boots to a shine. There was no hole in the wall. Not the slightest tear or blemish disfigured the smooth surface of the rose-strewn paper.

16

The approach of Christmas unsettled Adolf. He had nothing to contribute. He couldn't bear the tedious conversations centred on food and drink and seating arrangements. Alois and Meyer were involved in endless discussions concerning a goose they planned to buy. Every Friday the two men put money into a kitty towards its eventual purchase. Should they wait until Christmas Eve and pick up one cheap just as the street market was closing, or would they trust the word of the under-chef at the Adelphi who had promised to deliver a prime bird to the house on Christmas morning? What a disaster if he drank himself under the table the night before and never showed up! About the liquid refreshments they had no such worries. Kephalus wouldn't let them down. Being better off than either of them, he was providing the wine and some cheese. Along with the doctor, a woman called Mrs Prentice had been invited.

She, poor soul, would bring nothing apart from herself and four of her nine children. The festive meal would be devoured off the large scrubbed table in the cellar. 'I'm not sitting down with Kephalus,' cried Adolf when he heard.

'Good,' said Alois. 'Let us know when you're leaving.'

He was constructing darling Pat a little train on wheels. Adolf thought it a waste of time. Pat would only use it for a teething ring. Alois might as well hand him a block of wood and be done with it.

Not an evening passed without Meyer returning from the hotel, violin case bulging with supplies. Beaming, he spilled forth nuts and raisins and crystallised fruits and Havana cigars only a quarter smoked. Then Bridget, shrieking with pleasure and alarm, gathered up her precious materials out of harm's way. She was making the baby a new outfit. The table was spread from morning till night with pieces of calico and Scotch wincey and flannellette. Alois moaned perpetually about the cotton threads adhering to his coat. Finally, as soon as he stepped over the threshold he took to placing his hat inside a bag fashioned out of newspaper. He said it was damaging the pile, having to attack the brim so regularly with the clothes-brush.

The last Sunday before Christmas, Meyer asked Adolf if he would care to accompany Bridget and himself on an outing into the countryside. Bridget wanted to forage for pine boughs and holly, in order to decorate the front room; Adolf could search for chestnuts. He accepted. Though he would have liked to be alone with Meyer, anything was preferable to staying home with Alois, who was confined to bed with a chill. Alois had a nasty habit of tapping imperiously with his stick on the brass rail of the bed whenever he needed something. Adolf hated being at his beck and call and detested entering that intimate room with its great lump of a matrimonial bed, the lamp throwing a greenish light on to the ceiling, the combs and hairpins and jars of baby ointments scattered across the crocheted mats on the cheap dressing table. Unused to seeing Alois without his hat and coat, he found it difficult to keep a straight face at the sight of his stout brother comparatively naked, garbed in a frayed nightshirt, his plump neck still bearing the imprint of his collar stud as he lolled feverishly among the rumpled pillows or, desperate for a smoke, scrabbled in the wardrobe for the butt of a forgotten cigar, coughing as he bent over his pot belly, his shirt rising up above his muscular milk-white legs. Stripped of his fine clothes, his watch-chain and tie-pin, his silk scarf – now dangling from a nail behind the door – Alois was infantile and fractious. When he wasn't wheezing and whimpering he was calling out for sips of water, a clean handkerchief, a copy of the *Racing Gazette*. Adolf was tempted at such moments to pounce on him and stuff darling Pat's dummy down that open, demanding throat.

111

Bridget had intended to leave the baby with Mary O'Leary, but Meyer insisted that the fresh air would do him good.

'Fresh,' she said doubtfully. 'It'll turn his lungs to ice entirely.'

But she trusted Meyer's judgment. Before serving the Sunday dinner she toasted some bread at the fire and left it to harden. When she had washed up the pots on the landing, she put the bread and a container of water in a bag, along with her sewing scissors and an old motoring glove she had picked up in the street.

'You'd think we were off to the North Pole,' she said apologetically to Adolf, who was waiting impatiently at the window. She was worried in case Alois would set fire to the bedclothes while they were absent. 'Is it likely, do you think?' she asked Adolf.

He shrugged his shoulders. Though he wouldn't like Meyer to lose his property, he wouldn't have minded things getting hot for Alois.

They set off for Exchange Station, the two men dressed all in black and Bridget following behind, a tam o' shanter on her red hair and a black shawl of Mary O'Leary's bound tightly about her. Within its folds, encased from head to foot in woolly garments, the child was so closely strapped to its mother's body that he had little space to breathe, let alone howl.

'I think you will enjoy where we are going,' said Meyer.

'Sandhills and sea. The wind blowing through the pine trees. You are, after all, a country boy.'

'My formative years were spent in the city of Passau,' Adolf informed him. He didn't like being taken for a yokel. 'It wasn't until I was seven that my family moved to the country.'

'Ah,' Meyer said. 'That would explain your accent.'

'I'm not ashamed of my origins,' said Adolf stiffly.

When they reached the station and climbed into the comparative warmth of a third-class carriage, Bridget unwound darling Pat. He emerged scarlet in the face.

'You're right about the fresh air,' she told Meyer admiringly. 'Will you look at those cheeks.' And triumphantly she stood the baby on her knee and bounced him up and down.

The train pulled out of the station and moved in near darkness through fields of mud, caught between the river and the stagnant waters of the ship canal that cut inland to Manchester and the cotton mills of Lancashire.

Adolf thought the entire venture a mistake. They could have bought several Christmas trees in the market and garlanded the house with holly from top to bottom for the price Meyer had laid out on the tickets. He stared in disgust at the warehouses and the coal-yards and the stacks of timber rotting beside the railway track. From the chimneys of numerous ramshackle factories clouds of sulphurous smoke rolled under a sky so leaden and

113

uniformly grey it seemed to fit like a lid on the box of the earth beneath. Behind the industrial buildings and the meadows turned to rubbish tips, rows of back-to-back cottages sloped to the edge of the dock road.

'I have rarely seen such beautiful countryside,' he announced gloomily. 'It's breathtaking.'

'I expect it's too cold to paddle,' said Bridget, gazing complacently at the wretched view beyond the glass.

'All cities are alike,' Meyer said. 'Liverpool is no worse than any other metropolis. If you have heavy industry you have waste products and obsolete machinery. It's merely the miserable climate of this particular part of the world that accentuates the ugliness. If the sun was shining and the trees were in leaf, we would observe it quite differently. You, Adolphus, with your understanding of the Darwinist principles of the survival of the fittest will readily comprehend the necessity for all this.' And he pointed at the stunted bushes of elder and pussy willow that grew like clumps of tangled wire amid the sheets of corrugated iron and the sprawling mounds of brick.

'Flowers, Pat,' cried Bridget, staring intently at where Meyer pointed. Determined to see the crock of gold at the end of the rainbow, she held the baby up to the window and cried again: 'See the pretty flowers, Pat.'

However, once Seaforth was reached and the limits of the docks, the track curved inwards to the coast, until

114

finally the train puffed between fields of cabbages and potatoes and a strip of wind-blown heath bordered by hillocks of sand that dipped and rose upon a deserted beach. Then the sky lifted and white clouds rolled along the horizon.

'America,' said Adolf out loud, pressing his face to the carriage window and straining to catch the last glimpse of a dwindling ship that toppled on the edge of the sea. Beyond the stretch of black water lay the Atlantic ocean and the continent of Old Shatterhand himself.

'I have always been excited by the thought of the Americas,' remarked Meyer. 'I would like to have taken part in the Gold Rush.'

He turned to Bridget and asked: 'Tell me, do you think a country such as America, lacking as it must music and art and culture, is preferable to one's own?'

Bridget was acutely uncomfortable when Meyer talked to her like this. In the past she'd given herself a headache trying to work out his questions, only to find he didn't want any answers. It was baffling to her the way educated people like himself tormented themselves over books and paintings. You'd think wearing their eyes out reading and looking at the old things would be enough. Besides, her country was Ireland and, as everyone knew, between cutting the turf and following the gee-gees there wasn't a particle of time for messing with pictures. It hurt her jaw to sit there looking at him intelligently when she hadn't a thought in her head on the subject. Presently she told him: 'I have six cousins gone to Boston. And a brother who got off the ship and died while waiting to pass through the immigration.'

'It's a terrible thing,' suggested Meyer, 'to come face to face with freedom and opportunity.'

'It was terrible for me mammy,' said Bridget. 'Not knowing if he was buried decent.'

17

They alighted from the train at a small station some twelve miles from Liverpool. After the noise of the city the place was uncomfortably quiet. Apart from the ticket collector, and a donkey tied by a rope to a painted fence, there wasn't a soul in the world save themselves.

'Over there,' said Meyer, indicating a bicycle shed and a line of poplars blowing in the wind, 'there's a lane that cuts straight through to the woods and the shore.'

He insisted on carrying the child on his back. Fashioning a sling out of the black shawl, he tied the ends about his waist. The baby laid its cheek against his coat and sucked drowsily at its woollen fist. Locking his hands behind him to support the slumped bundle of darling Pat, Meyer galloped energetically past the bicycle shed and turned the corner.

'Isn't he good with the children?' said Bridget.

Stumbling over the words, Adolf told her that in his

opinion men without families were often more sensitive to the young.

'He's a son of his own,' Bridget said, 'somewhere or other. And a wife living in the Midlands.' She flew ahead, red hair blowing about her red cheeks, anxious to keep the child under surveillance.

Confused by this startling piece of information, Adolf remained rooted to the spot. He had no idea what the Midlands might be. Was it possible that the generous, milk-of-kindness Meyer had abandoned his wife in a field? Perhaps in his references to obsolete machinery and waste products he had been alluding to Frau Meyer.

'Hurry, hurry,' called Bridget, dodging briskly round the corner of the shed.

Deep in thought, Adolf followed. He came into a cobbled yard fronted by a public house with shuttered windows. Set to one side was a wicket gate leading to a cinder path running black as a river through a water-logged field and a coal-yard fenced with poplars. In the distance he was in time to see Meyer and Bridget closing a second, larger gate. He shouted, but evidently they couldn't hear him. As he watched they scurried up a slight rise, Meyer hump-backed under his burden and Bridget apparently scrambling on all fours as she endeavoured to keep up with him. Then the ground dipped and they fell out of sight.

Whistling to show he didn't care, Adolf sauntered

through the wicket gate and along the path. There were crows stalking the hills of slack behind the trees. At the sound of his slithering boots they rose with outstretched wings and circled like vultures. He was damned if he was going to break into a sprint to catch up with his sister-in-law and Meyer. Obviously it wasn't to be one of those gentle afternoon strolls enlivened by conversation and a study of nature. They had set out too late. If only Alois hadn't whined for his dinner – already mist was beginning to seep across the flat meadows of sodden grass.

Upon arriving at the second gate he was surprised to find it wouldn't open. He shoved without success. It was tied to a post by wire so rusted and fiercely entwined that he was forced to clamber over the bars. Spreadeagled along the topmost slat, he had a clear view of the bleak landscape ahead. An uneven stretch of waste ground, edged by a thin avenue of pines, tapered to a blur of trees on the horizon. He heard what he took to be the dull roar of waves breaking on a far-off shore. There were no winding streams or wooded hollows, no hedgerows thick with winter berries. He couldn't think why Meyer had imagined he would enjoy such a desolate, moaning place. Save for that line of black firs he was alone on a blasted heath under a sky so vast and stormy he was no bigger than an insect on the moss-stained bars of the gate. Below him at the base of the post writhed slugs, slippery as fish among the rotting

119

strands of grass. Shuddering, he slid to the muddy earth and cupping his hands about his mouth shouted again. This time he was answered.

Entering the crackling shadows of the pines he found Meyer examining the trunk of a tree. Bridget was kneeling dishevelled on the ground, giving darling Pat sips of water out of the container.

'There you are,' said Meyer, as if Adolf had been deliberately elusive. 'What kept you?'

'I'm no good at running,' said Adolf.

'Always the lone wolf,' cried Meyer jovially.

'The gate was fast shut,' Adolf said, growing red in the face.

'It was bound with wire,' suggested Meyer.

'And yet I saw you open it. Or rather, I saw you close it.'

'It would be more correct to say we went through it,' said Meyer.

Adolf stared at him.

'Wriggled,' explained Meyer. 'Between the bars.'

I'm not blind, thought Adolf. Nor did he think that Meyer, resembling as he had done the Hunchback of Notre Dame, could have squeezed through two slabs of butter, let alone a five-bar gate.

They continued on their way, Meyer carrying the shopping bag and Bridget the baby. At intervals Meyer stopped to gather pine cones and to consult his watch.

It didn't seem likely that they would find a holly bush within a hundred miles.

Gradually the trees became more numerous. The low booming of the sea grew louder. They stumbled at last through a forest so dense that the sky was blotted out. The child, small face shimmering like a pearl in the green dusk, clung solemn-eyed to his mother's neck.

'Not much further,' said Meyer, and holding up his arm to ward off the webs of spiders slung from branch to branch he guided Bridget through the gloaming.

They emerged on to a path leading to an ancient church ringed with tall elms and bounded by a wall of crumbling stone. Adolf realised that they were still some distance from the sea. The roaring he had continually heard in his ears was no more than the wind blowing in the lofty branches of the pines.

Again Meyer consulted his watch. 'We haven't a great deal of time,' he said. 'If I remember rightly there are holly bushes behind the church.'

Eagerly Bridget trotted forward, the baby bobbing on her hip.

Meyer stood on the path, shoulders slumped; a grey cobweb drifted from the brim of his black felt hat. He stared wearily in the direction of the unseen road masked by the high wall and the ragged elms.

'You are tired,' said Adolf. 'Stay here and rest. I'll accompany Bridget.'

121

'On the contrary,' said Meyer selflessly. 'It is you who must stay here. I'll attend to Frau Hitler. You explore the church. There are many interesting architectural features. It was built in the twelfth century.' Standing at Adolf's elbow he indicated the squat Norman tower.

'Come with me,' urged Adolf. 'One cannot always be at the beck and call of women.'

'True,' murmured Meyer. 'But then I am in possession of the scissors.'

'I'll take them to her,' said Adolf, and he held out his hand for the shopping bag.

'You are not suitably equipped for hacking wood,' pointed out Meyer. 'You have no gloves.' It seemed he was determined to sacrifice himself.

At that instant a man's head, wearing a checked cap and trailing a strip of white cloth like a pig-tail, floated horizontally and disembodied above the churchyard wall. As Adolf gazed open-mouthed at this apparition, the head drew level with a wooden gate and he saw a man on a bicycle flash past, his two-tone golfing shoes whirling round and round as he pedalled furiously down the lane. Meyer, who was now walking away, didn't appear to have noticed anything out of the ordinary. Before Adolf had time to call out, the checked cap had vanished altogether and Meyer was swallowed up among the trees.

18

Adolf spent a depressing ten minutes trying to gain entrance to the church. It wasn't his day for opening doors or gates. Testily he kicked at the massive oval of wood studded with nails. Recoiling, he curled his stubbed toes within his boot and hopped up and down, cursing. The pain was terrible. Removing his boot he fingered his worn sock and was relieved to find he wasn't bleeding. Had he known how to reach the station he would have left there and then. The foolish whims of his sister-in-law were none of his business. Obviously Meyer was too weak and sentimental to order her to forage for her own Christmas greenery. Let them shop together like the peasants they undoubtedly were. Thoroughly irritated by Meyer's indiscriminate attentions to others, he stumbled from the porch, boot in hand, and hobbled round the back of the church. He distinctly heard voices and the breaking of twigs. Coming to a gap in the thick hedge of briars he fought his way into the forest beyond. He didn't wish Bridget and Meyer to wander so far that he would lose touch with them entirely.

He had only travelled a short distance when he became aware of someone behind him, blundering through the undergrowth. He spun round and listened. For a moment he thought he glimpsed the white blob of Pat's woollen bonnet, but it was only a bird's feather drifting from the darkness above. Cautiously he walked on. Again he heard those unmistakable sounds of pursuit. Careless of the branches that plucked his hair and tore at his clothing, he began to run deeper into the woods. He didn't know why he was so afraid. Once he glanced over his shoulder and saw, fragmented by trees, the figure of the man on the bicycle, bare-headed now, the strip of cloth dangling over one ear as, fleet-footed as an Ogellalah Indian, he tracked him through the pines.

Suddenly the ground sloped upwards. A broken bough, pointed like a spear, jabbed Adolf in the ribs. Grunting, he reached the edge of the rise and toppled into a hollow lined with blown sand and pine-needles. With his last ounce of strength he raised one arm and lobbed his boot blindly into the trees. A patch of white sky rocked above him as the branches shifted in the wind. There was no escape. Defenceless, he awaited the stranger's approach.

'My dear boy,' exclaimed Meyer, looking down at him with an expression of concern, 'have you injured yourself?'

'I have no need of self-inflicted wounds,' said Adolf, struggling to regain his composure. 'Not when everyone else is determined to harm me. I am perpetually stalked by unknown enemies.'

'What has happened to your shoe?' said Meyer.

'I have suffered enough,' Adolf cried. 'They are everywhere. On boats, beside railway tracks, outside picture houses, smiling above beards. Just now there was another with a bandage about his head.'

'Another what?' asked Meyer, bewildered.

'Another man,' Adolf said. 'Less than a week ago he leapt through the roses in the top room of your house.'

'Through the roses—'

'I'm distraught,' admitted Adolf. 'But I'm not stupid. I can put two and two together.'

Meyer lowered himself on to the rim of the slope and stared thoughtfully at the ground. 'You are telling me a bearded man wearing a bandage jumped through some flowers—'

'No,' said Adolf. 'He was clean-shaven. He came through the wall. Later he wore your golfing shoes, the ones I saw in the wardrobe. Brown and white—'

'Brown and white?' repeated Meyer. He flung up his arms in despair. 'Do I look like a man who plays golf?'

'Be that as it may,' said Adolf darkly, 'first he was on a bicycle and then he was on foot.'

'He came through the wall on a bicycle?' Meyer said.

Furious at this evasive conversation, Adolf attempted to stand up. His legs were so weak he felt they would snap under his weight. He succeeded merely in crouching on all fours like a dog.

'Lie down,' advised Meyer. 'Lie down and breathe deeply.'

Adolf rolled sideways and lay with his knees drawn up to his chest.

Presently he murmured: 'There are several men following me. Some are bearded, some are not. There was a man in the square whom I thought I recognised. I spoke to him, imagining we had met before. It may be he was on the channel steamer. He stole my cap.'

'Who has stolen your boot?' demanded Meyer.

'No one,' said Adolf. 'My boot is only mislaid.'

After some moments of silence, Meyer asked: 'Why are all these men following you? Are you in trouble with the police?'

'Certainly not,' protested Adolf. 'It is Alois who has criminal tendencies, not I.' He sat up and shook the sand from his hair. 'I am the innocent victim of a failure in postal communications.' It was unmanly of him, he felt, to confide in Meyer, but he could no longer keep his fears to himself. Assuming it was curiosity and not pity that caused the older man to watch him so attentively, he endeavoured to explain his position. 'When I first left Linz for Vienna I notified the authorities of my new address. I realised I would soon be eligible for military service—'

'Ah! Now I understand,' said Meyer, with irritating perception.

'Allow me to finish,' cried Adolf. 'You are jumping to conclusions. In giving my change of address I was acting with the utmost correctness. Unfortunately I didn't have the same address for very long, or any other address for that matter. Circumstances forced me to spend the next few years wandering the city like a tramp. I can't be blamed.'

'My dear Adolphus,' Meyer said. 'It is obvious to me that your dreadful experiences in Vienna have temporarily affected your natural good sense. If the authorities pursued every young man who avoided military service, they would bankrupt themselves in no time. In any event they would be unlikely to follow you on bicycles.'

'I avoided nothing,' shouted Adolf. 'I received no letter or documents. The postman doesn't deliver mail to doss houses or park benches.' In his annoyance he raked the ground with his fingers and sent a shower of sand into one eye. 'Damn and blast,' he moaned.

'Quite,' said Meyer soothingly. 'It wasn't your fault. I'm convinced your particular state of mind primarily arises from frustration. You are essentially an artist and by that I do not necessarily mean you are a painter. Such a temperament can be expressed in many activities.'

Eyes painfully watering, Adolf blinked up at him. Though gratified by Meyer's recognition of his artistic abilities, he still smouldered under the earlier implication that he was a coward.

'At the moment,' continued Meyer, 'you are poisoned – one might almost say opulently swollen – by creative urges that have no outlet.'

'Indeed,' said Adolf. He looked doubtfully at his thin wrists protruding from the sleeves of his second-hand coat.

'What is more,' Meyer said, 'you can't be blamed for imagining you were being hunted. Had I known you were quite so distressed I would have taken you into my confidence. The man with the bandage round his head is an acquaintance of Kephalus and myself. His name is Michael Murphy. He can have no possible interest in you. Indeed it is he who is being followed.'

'By whom?' asked Adolf. 'And for what reason?'

'It is a private matter. Between Mr Murphy and the police. I can say no more.'

Adolf experienced a profound sense of relief. Though it was already late afternoon and the sky was the colour of ashes, he could have sworn he felt the warmth of the sun on his neck. He smiled broadly. But for inhibitions he would, out of sheer gratitude, have embraced Meyer on both cheeks.

'And those others,' he enquired. 'The ones with beards. Are they also wanted by the police?'

'Now there,' replied Meyer regretfully, 'I cannot help you. I have no knowledge of any persons, bearded or otherwise, who may be following you.' The subject seemed closed. He was anxious to return and find Bridget.

Thinking it over, Adolf comforted himself with the thought that there could be no smoke without fire. If Meyer consorted with criminals then his house was bound to be under surveillance. It was Meyer who was being watched, not himself.

They wasted some time looking for the thrown-away boot.

Finally Meyer insisted that the search should be abandoned: the evening mist would be bad for the child's chest.

When eventually they struggled through the hedge into the churchyard, Adolf was not surprised to discover that Bridget had been unsuccessful in her hunt for holly bushes. She too was probably acquainted with the wounded Michael Murphy. Though it would hardly keep the body and soul of a sparrow together, he had seen her secrete three portions of toast inside her shopping bag before leaving the house. He passed no moral judgments on either Murphy or his fellow conspirators. He felt equal contempt for the underdog and the forces of law and order. It amused him, however, to think of Alois, so desperately courting respectability, unknowingly enmeshed in a tangle of shady dealings and secret intrigues. Every

129

time he opened his pigskin suitcase full of those damnable razor blades someone, God willing, was loitering in a doorway taking down notes in shorthand or watching him through binoculars.

They filed out of the churchyard and into the road.

Adolf offered to carry darling Pat to the station. Bridget made various comical references to his stockinged foot. She said he was a terrible man for losing things and she'd never forgive him if he misplaced the baby.

With Pat safely snuggled against his breast, Adolf wondered what Meyer had in mind when he had hinted that there were many outlets for a creative personality. Architecture was out of the question. He didn't have sufficient grades to sit for entrance to the university. It was surely too late for him to learn an instrument. He didn't have the stomach to be a doctor. Perhaps dealing with people was his forte – after all he had been someone of influence among the occupants of the various homes for the destitute in which he had stayed.

It was pleasant to hold the warm child in his arms. Pat's moist, accepting smile brought tears to his eyes. His anxieties over the last few weeks had affected him more than he had realised – now, freed from demons, he was filled with emotion. The fields which earlier had stretched drably to the horizon now appeared appropriately seasonal and but for the absence of snow worthy of a painting by Breughel. He was astonished at the tenderness evoked by the sight of Bridget's shoulders hunched in her shabby coat as she marched gamely ahead; a bunch of her hair, escaping from beneath the knitted tam o' shanter, rippled like a flag in the darkening lane. He was homesick; yet he had no home to go to. All the way to the railway station he held the shawl carefully at an angle so as to screen the baby from the damp night air. He was disproportionately hurt when Bridget failed to remark that he too was good with children.

19

Two days before Christmas, while Bridget was out shopping, Adolf took a square of card from the inside of a biscuit tin and propping Pat in his high chair began to draw him. He was delighted with his efforts. He felt that the sketch had a delicacy of line totally in accord with its subject. The dimple on the right cheek could have been more subtle, but there was something little short of miraculous in the shading of the left eyelid. When the drawing was finished Adolf placed it inside a newspaper and hid it under the couch, together with a book he intended giving to Meyer. The book was a life of Mozart, bound in leather. Adolf had procured it from the reading room of the public library. Taking two volumes from the shelves he had sat down at the table provided, making sure that he cleared his throat loudly enough for the official behind the desk to notice him. Half an hour later he had slipped one book inside his coat and secured it under his armpit. Pushing back his chair, he had made a fearful racket in standing up and returning the remaining volume to the shelf. He could tell by the pinched look on the librarian's face as he went out of the door that he was glad to see the back of him.

All the way to Stanhope Street he walked with his arms held tightly to his sides like a military man. Only when he was safe indoors – and even then he turned his back on the windows overlooking the dance hall – did he remove his overcoat. He wasn't sure what to do about a present for Alois. He had tried to perfect the piece of metal intended as a gramophone handle, but he lacked the tool needed to cut the thread correctly. Besides, he didn't want to provoke Alois who, unwrapping such a gift, might possibly receive it in a less than Christian spirit and use it for a purpose not actually meant. He didn't want to be brained for his trouble. As an afterthought, he retrieved the drawing from under the couch and wrote across one corner: 'To Bridget and Alois Hitler, with regards from A. Hitler. Liverpool. December, 1912.'

At midday on Christmas Eve he was called downstairs to the basement and put to work scraping potatoes and chopping the brown bits out of the brussels sprouts. Darling Pat, looking like a little old man at the barber's, a towel tucked about his fat neck, sat in a chair pulled to the table, thwacking with a wooden spoon at links of sausages coiled on a newspaper. There were basins overflowing with forcemeat, with chestnut stuffing, with jellies not yet set. A jug of buttermilk stood amid lemon peel and chicken livers and lumps of dripping. Each time Pat jabbed downwards with his spoon a quantity of shallots and several damp cigars rolled back and forth across the table. But for the unhygienic conditions and the abandoned way in which Mary O'Leary manned the sink, bailing water as if the basement was listing, the amount of provisions would not have disgraced the kitchens of the Adelphi Hotel. The air was thick with the mingled smells of soap and pastry, blood and tangerines. In the absence of holly, Bridget had secured paper chains from the lamp above the table to the clothes rack over the range. So intense was the heat and so great the activity that at regular intervals the loops broke from their moorings and one strand or another whipped across the table and trailed on the floor. 'It's not for me,' Bridget confided whenever this disaster occurred. 'It's Mrs Prentice's children I'm thinking of, poor souls.' And standing on a rickety chair she attached the paper ends once more, now bearing droplets of buttermilk or globs of stuffing and stained brown from the smear of chicken livers.

Adolf resented the way the women treated him as incompetent. Hadn't he cooked the meals for his sister Paula when his mother was ill? Numerous times Bridget or Mary O'Leary sent him out on trivial errands – to buy a twist of salt, to have the knives sharpened, to see if the publican over the road would lend them empty barrels for the children to sit on – but when the moment came to fetch home the piece of ham roasting in the baker's oven Mary O'Leary threw a shawl over her bonnet and prepared to go herself. She spoke to Bridget across him, as though he wasn't there. 'He'll only break a leg,' she said. 'Or lose the dish, or fall down a manhole.' He sulked in a corner and stared gloomily at the Christmas tree propped in a bucket against the wall, its branches threaded with tinsel and hung about with chocolate pennies wrapped in silver paper.

'Will you stop scrowling,' said Bridget firmly. 'You'll turn the milk.'

'Mary O'Leary returned with the ham and with Mrs Prentice, who wore a man's cap and an old flannel shirt over layers of bedraggled skirts. Against all odds she was apparently cheerful, for upon being introduced to Adolf she squeezed his arm familiarly and bellowed with laughter. When she saw the food on the table she pressed her hand to her shapeless breast as if her heart might fall out with the shock.

'Jesus!' she cried. 'You'se gone overboard and no mistake.'

'There's things for the children,' Bridget said. 'Little things, mind. Nothing to write home about.' She had

135

made a rag doll for the youngest girl and hemmed a handkerchief for each of the others – though God knows, judging by the usual state of the children, they'd never understand what they were for. It had been Meyer's idea to invite Mrs Prentice. As he was providing most of the food, Bridget wasn't in a position to argue. She fully intended to scrub darling Pat from head to foot with carbolic soap, once the party was over.

'God will bless you,' promised Mrs Prentice, wiping away a happy tear with the ragged cuff of her sleeve. She wasn't stopping; she was off to see her Elsie in Chatham Street. Elsie was expecting again and low in spirits. Every time she coughed she thought her whole caboodle was dropping out. She wouldn't forget to bring the cards. She spoke in such a strange tongue and screwed her face up to such an extent that Adolf wondered if she were sane. When she was leaving she squeezed his arm again and shouted in a voice like a derisive trumpet: 'Tarra, lamb-chop.'

By the end of the afternoon Adolf was worn out. He had tried to restore a little cleanliness and order to the basement. Several times he had brushed the floor clear of debris only to have Mary O'Leary wantonly fling down potato peelings and leftovers. He fitted a piece of muslin over the jug of buttermilk and gathered up the news-papers in an attempt to wash down the table.

Pat howled so much at the removal of the sausages

that Bridget made Adolf put them back. 'He's doing no harm,' she said. 'Let him batter them with his old spoon.'

When Adolf protested that they wouldn't be fit to eat, she tossed her head and told him that until such time as he paid for the food Pat could put them through the mangle for all she cared. Angrily he stalked out of the kitchen and went upstairs to lie on the couch.

When he woke it was dark and Bridget was preparing the child for bed.

'Are you coming to midnight mass later?' she asked. 'Or will you stay home with Pat?'

'I will rest here,' he decided.

'Here, take him,' she said, and dumping Pat on to the sofa she struggled through into the bedroom carrying the bottom drawer of the wardrobe. The baby was tired. He keeled over and lay with his cheek resting trustingly on Adolf's shoulder. They yawned together, lying there with the lamp hissing on the table. When Bridget came and took him away, Adolf missed him.

'I have a cousin,' said Bridget, some minutes later when she was tidying the table. 'She's younger than me. I was thinking you should meet her.'

'I don't understand,' Adolf said, peering over the edge of the plaid blanket.

'My cousin,' she repeated. 'A young lady. I thought it would be nice for you to meet her.'

'I am too busy to meet young ladies,' he said.

'I can see that,' said Bridget tartly. The nerve of him, lying there like Lord Muck, pretending he was a working man.

She took her coat down from the peg of the hat-stand, preferring to sit downstairs with Mary O'Leary until it was time to go round the corner to the church. Meyer and Alois wouldn't be back until the small hours of the morning; Christmas Eve was a good night for picking up tips, and the management always sent them home with an extra three shillings in their wages. When the last of the residents had retired to bed, the staff usually had a knees-up in the store room. She was about to march out without a word when something in Adolf's expression made her hesitate. He looked haughty and yet bereft. Was he blinking his eyelids to hold back tears?

'Do you need anything to eat?' she asked.

'No, thank you,' he said.

'You don't care much for Christmas, do you?'

He shook his head. Sitting up and throwing off the rug, he began to put on his old boots.

'I don't suppose you like dancing either?'

'No,' he said. 'I'm not a man for dancing.'

'Alois loves dancing. He likes parties and people. Sometimes I think the razor blades will be the ruin of him. He'd be better off sticking with the catering business. He likes nothing better than to inspect the tables and hear the band strike up.'

'At Christmas,' said Adolf awkwardly, 'my mother died.'

'Ah God!' cried Bridget. 'I didn't know that. Alois never said.'

'She was not his mother.'

'He was very fond of her,' protested Bridget. 'He always said she was a good mother to him. Between you, me and the gatepost, for all he goes on about the old fella I think he liked *her* best.'

'When we were small,' confided Adolf, 'my mother called my father Uncle.'

'That's queer,' said Bridget.

'She was young,' Adolf said. 'Also she was his niece.'

'Get away,' cried Bridget. 'The priest would never have allowed it.'

Adolf's English wasn't sufficient for him to explain that his father had obtained a dispensation from the Pope. Besides, Bridget was looking longingly at the door, anxious to be gone. He would have liked to have given her the drawing of Pat – now, with Alois out of the way – but he supposed she was in too much of a hurry. Perhaps he would never show it to her. Already her hand was on the latch of the door.

'It's a grand time of the year, isn't it?' she said, trying to cover her escape with words. 'Everyone's in a fine humour and the men are falling over themselves to be nice.'

Adolf managed a bleak smile. Then she was on to the

139

landing and running down the stairs as if the place was on fire. I haven't always been a wet blanket, he thought. There had been moments, certainly as a boy, when he had made his mother smile.

He spent his evening lying on the couch, propped on pillows, watching the couples in the dance hall opposite. Now and then a rumpus broke out. Some word or foot out of place and a tornado of figures, arms flailing beneath the drifting streamers, whirled up suddenly from the centre of the throng. The dancers, shrieking, scattered to the walls. Shoulder to shoulder the bouncers charged. Grappling with the troublemakers, they partnered them one by one in a spirited polka to the doors. The combatants, booted into the night, continued to lash out at one another until someone called from a doorway that the scuffers were coming.

Shortly before midnight, a woman pushing a handcart hurled a three-legged stool through the glass panel of the saloon door.

20

On Christmas morning, Bridget gave Adolf a handkerchief made out of the same material as his brown shirt.
At one corner she had embroidered his initials in white
thread.

Hastily he pushed the drawing into her hand.

'It's him,' she cried, impressed by his cleverness.

'Let's see,' Alois demanded, snatching the card from
her. Liverish from the previous night's excesses, he
slumped over the table in vest and braces. He examined
the drawing carefully.

'More than anything else,' he said at last, 'it resembles
a potato.'

The Christmas dinner began at five o'clock. During
the earlier part of the afternoon Alois and Kephalus sat
with Meyer in his room and drank cherry brandy. Adolf
stayed downstairs with the women. Since dawn, Mary
O'Leary had been cooking the goose. The basement was

now in a fair state of order with the table laid and the floor swept. Bridget had hung the remainder of the brown cloth over the worst of the vegetable growths by the door. The candles were lit on the Christmas tree. Mrs Prentice's children, dressed in various articles of clothing, some too small and some too large for them, stood overwhelmed at the far end of the table. The landlord of the public house, made contrary by the wrecking of his door, had changed his mind about loaning the barrels. Adolf had retrieved the three-legged stool abandoned in the gutter.

'They don't need nothing to park on,' said Mrs Prentice, gaudy in a sateen jacket of shot purple. 'The meat will go down safer if they'se stand up.'

When the men were called for the meal, it seemed there were a hundred people in the kitchen, barging into chairs and upsetting buckets, littering the table with glasses and bottles. A great deal of kissing and playful slapping was indulged in by Kephalus when greeting the children. They accepted his attentions without flinching, eyes unwaveringly and hopelessly fixed on the spitting goose, bursting with stuffing, being lifted from the smoke-filled oven by Mary O'Leary.

The doctor wanted to separate the children and string them like beads among the company, but Meyer said it would spoil their appetites; he settled them cross-legged on the stone floor with their backs to the wall and gave the eldest boy, Gordon, a cup of beer. Everyone agreed the young had an astonishing time of it now, what with health and public education and generally being treated as persons of some importance. The boy sipping his drink, who was nearly thirteen, had been employed for two years, according to Mrs Prentice, in the soap works in Blundell Street and wasn't allowed to work after seven o'clock at night. When she thought of her own brother at half Gordon's age, ferreting up and down chimneys and having the brine rubbed into his knees so that he wouldn't bleed too much when climbing between the bricks, she thanked God for the decent times they were living in.

Mary O'Leary had set an extra place next to her own. When Meyer asked her to pass the plate, she said dismally, 'No need. It's an empty gesture.' Overwhelmed, she bowed her head in its withered bonnet.

'There, there,' cried Meyer, putting down his knife and going to her. Gently he patted her shoulder.

After a moment Mary O'Leary recovered and wiped her perspiring face with the edge of the tablecloth. When the wine was poured, Adolf held up his glass, determined to be congenial. Seated as he was beside the sickening Kephalus, he felt he would need something to blur his sensibilities. The doctor, garbed like a cockroach in a black frock-coat glazed with age, ate as if he was at the horse-trough. Mrs Prentice sought a diagnosis of her Elsie's delicate condition. Pinned between Kephalus's

143

elbows and Mrs Prentice's purple bosom, Adolf was unable to detach himself altogether from the medical details. He drank as much as he was able in as short a time as possible.

When most of the eating was done, Mrs Prentice's girl, Dolly, was called upon to sing.

'No, no,' she whined, pressing herself against the mildewed wall.

Her mother rose from the table and staggering slightly jerked the child to her feet. Dolly was lifted on to the three-legged stool, where she stood with her stubby toes poking out of the worn uppers of her button boots, her cheeks flushing pink from terror and excitement. Not a peep came out of her.

'Leave the poor girl alone,' cried Bridget, as the men struck the table encouragingly with their pudding spoons.

But Mrs Prentice wasn't prepared to let the matter rest. After some whispered words in Dolly's ear and a somewhat vicious pinching of the meagre flesh on her arm, the child fixed her eyes on some point above the hanging lamp and stretching forth a bony finger sang quaveringly: 'The boy I love is up in the gallery . . .'

When she had finished she jumped from the stool to tumultuous applause and collapsed on the floor among her brothers and sisters like a puppet whose strings had been cut.

'Even as a babby,' boasted Mrs Prentice, 'in a gown

made out of a sugar bag our Dolly warbled shriller than a nightingale.'

Alois proposed a series of toasts, first to Dolly for her performance, then to Herr Meyer for making such a feast possible, and lastly to absent and seafaring friends.

On hearing this last proposal Mary O'Leary heaved herself upright and drained her glass at one gulp.

Meyer remained seated, eyes gazing sombrely at the debris of his Christmas pudding.

When the women and children began to clear the pots from the table, the men brought out their cigars and lighting them blew clouds of smoke at the stained ceiling. Adolf slumped sideways in his chair. He couldn't stop smiling.

'You have thrown off your mantle of gloom,' observed Meyer. 'A drink has brought you out of yourself.'

'I've been out of myself before now,' confided Adolf. 'I could astonish you.' Laying a hand on Meyer's arm to steady himself, he asked in a confused and rambling fashion if his friend had seen Wagner's opera *Rienzi*.

'Yes,' said Meyer, 'I have.'

'I saw it with my friend Gustl,' said Adolf. 'I found the story of the rise and fall of a tribune of Rome particularly . . . particularly . . .'

'Apt? In a quarter of the city which was inhabited by mechanics and Jews – if I may quote the historian – the marriage of an innkeeper and a washerwoman produced the future deliverer of Rome,' said Meyer helpfully.

'Hold your tongue,' Adolf said. 'Suffocated by the smoke of cigars in the foyer I left the theatre after the performance and climbed a steep hill outside the town. Crouching in the wet grass, I waited.' He stared thoughtfully at Meyer's neckcloth.

'For whom?' asked Meyer.

At that moment Adolf's thoughts, which previously had been sluggish and conflicting, became lucid and capable of being expressed in words. Moreover he felt a pressing need to communicate. Pushing back his chair, he rose to his feet.

'Young Adolf's going to make a speech,' cried Alois, stamping his boots on the stone floor to attract the attention of the doctor, who was engaged in throwing bonbons at the children.

'Waiting is a tedious business,' said Adolf, addressing the door of the coal cellar. 'Long ago I had faced that optical illusion of the looking-glass and seen the ignoble reflection totally at variance with the image of the true, inner self—'

'What's he talking about?' demanded Alois.

'Long ago I had dismissed it for the distortion it was. But that night, that night in the grass, shivering with cold and emotion, I made a conscious effort to detach myself from this puny body, these brittle bones, this . . . this . . .' Here Adolf pressed his fingers to the bridge of his nose and hesitated.

'Lump,' suggested Alois.

'Fragile brain,' continued Adolf, unaware of the interruption. 'Straining in every fibre I crouched there, panting. I heard the dew sliding down each stalk of grass, felt the motion of the earth as it turned through space. I sought to fuse my spirit with those of the dead tribunes of Rome, with the immortal music of Wagner. I felt at that minute as if the planets changed their courses and the rivers ran with blood.'

He was extending one arm towards the ceiling now, eyes staring and intent, as though he saw through the plaster and the beams, the rooms above, the roof itself, and gazed upon the stars. Alois, who throughout this tirade had interjected various humorous remarks relating to defecating in the grass and haemorrhoids, fell silent. Bridget, unable to understand one word in ten, trembled as if her life was in danger.

'During the grub years of my miserable childhood,' thundered Adolf, 'and during the miserable caterpillar years of my young manhood when I was repeatedly denied entrance to the Academy, I held fast to the belief that one day I would undergo a metamorphosis of the spirit. On that cold hillside my patience was rewarded. Had I not long since renounced the faith of my boyhood, I would have compared my exalted state to that of Christ's in the Garden of Gethsemane. It is useless to denounce such an experience as adolescent and commonplace. That

147

night I struggled free from from the dusty membranes of both grub and caterpillar and emerged finally, an airborne creature soaring on iridescent wings above the earth.'

For several seconds Adolf remained standing, arm raised in that salute to the heavens. Beads of perspiration trickled down his cheeks.

Then abruptly he sat down. Misjudging the position of his chair he fell to the floor and disappeared under the table.

'That was nice,' said Mrs Prentice. 'Is he going to be a priest, then?' Until hearing the word 'Christ' she had been under the impression she was listening to a foreign, more dramatic rendering of 'The Boy I Love is Up in the Gallery.'

No one answered her. Mary O'Leary, who had left off stacking the plates, clattered the saucepans into the sink.

'I was right,' said Kephalus thoughtfully. He leaned across and whispered to Meyer: 'Undoubtedly an hysteric.' Leaving the table he went out into the front area for a breath of night air.

Wearing an expression of mingled admiration and disgust, Alois peered under the cloth at his half-brother, before following the doctor out of the scullery door.

'What was he on about?' asked Bridget, vexed. 'He's put a damper on the proceedings.'

'Bugs,' said Mary O'Leary. 'Flying insects and bugs.'

148

Recovering, Adolf climbed slowly to his feet and sat down. He sighed once, twice, as if his heart was heavy. Under the gaslight his face was so wan as to appear green.

'Do you often have such experiences?' asked Meyer.

'No,' said Adolf. 'Where is your son?'

21

Some time later, after Meyer had helped him into the back yard and encouraged him to vomit down a drain, Adolf apologised for his curiosity.

'The fault is mine,' said Meyer. 'Don't mention it.'

'Doorman?' queried Adolf, leaning weakly against the wall of the house. 'At the theatre?'

'Yes,' said Meyer. 'Behind the market.'

Adolf begged his forgiveness. He hadn't meant to pry again.

'I should,' conceded Meyer, 'have confided in you earlier. But then it is not something to shout from the rooftops.'

'Quite,' said Adolf. 'You may rely on me.'

Escorting him to the kitchen, Meyer went upstairs to find Kephalus. They were taking three of Mrs Prentice's children home before going on to visit an acquaintance of the doctor. The youngest child, clutching the rag doll, was asleep across two chairs. In a generous moment, already regretted, Alois had said he would stay behind with his wife for an hour or so. She had gone to put darling Pat in his drawer. Alois sat fretting by the fire, a towel draped over his lap to protect his trousers from Mary O'Leary and Mrs Prentice who, in a slap-dash way, were still removing pots from the oven and generally continuing to tidy up the kitchen.

'You made an exhibition of yourself,' he said crossly to Adolf. 'I'm tired of your sly innuendoes. It's not seemly to speak of one's father in such a manner.'

'What innuendoes?' asked Adolf, astonished. 'I never mentioned him.'

'Miserable childhood!' said Alois. 'Herr Meyer was scandalised, I could tell.'

'Not by me,' retorted Adolf. 'It was your stupid reference to sailors that upset him.'

Alois looked baffled.

'His son,' said Adolf. 'The only one to be saved.'

'What are you talking about now?' demanded Alois.

'The article in the newspaper. At the very bottom of the column. Dressed in a petticoat and a shawl, he jumped into the lifeboat.'

'You're mad,' said Alois. 'You shouldn't drink.'

'At least I didn't remind him of it,' shouted Adolf. 'I didn't propose a toast to absent and seafaring friends.'

Alois leapt to his feet and throwing the towel into the hearth went to the basement door.

'You're off, then,' said Mary O'Leary with satisfaction.

'Tell Frau Hitler,' shouted Alois, 'that I was driven into the night by my demented brother.' He ran up the area steps to the street.

Adolf was left alone with the women. He felt it impolite of Meyer to have deserted him, particularly after accepting the gift of the library book. To his knowledge, Alois had given Meyer nothing. He said haltingly to Bridget, when she returned: 'Did they not think to include me?'

'They've gone drinking,' said Mary O'Leary. 'You haven't the capacity. One more drink and you'd fall in the Mersey.' She was speaking no more than the truth. He was still walking unsteadily.

Adolf wasn't unduly upset at remaining behind. Despite its squalor, the warm kitchen, still fragrant with the smells of meat and pudding, reminded him of home. He preferred the company of women, even such doubtful specimens as the hirsute Mary O'Leary. While outwardly she treated him with contempt, he sensed her protectiveness towards him: she didn't want him drowned. And now, Mrs Prentice was laying a pack of cards on the table. He would enjoy a game of cards. At the Männerheim, one long cold winter, they had played almost every evening. The stakes weren't high – a cup of coffee, yesterday's newspaper, the loan of an extra blanket for two nights. Sometimes he'd won.

He sat expectantly at the table.

'Couldn't you keep an ear on the baby?' asked Bridget, wanting him out of the way.

He pretended he hadn't understood. He wasn't a nursemaid. To his disgust, he found that Mrs Prentice merely intended to indulge in fortune telling. Yet he stayed where he was, held by the absurd anxiety on Bridget's face as Mrs Prentice shuffled the pack. She dealt a king of clubs and a hand of hearts and diamonds. Bridget smiled with relief.

Adolf could make little sense of anything that was said. The women nudged each other and could hardly speak for laughing. Once Mrs Prentice dropped a card to the floor and Mary O'Leary picked it up. When she saw that it was the ace of spades she screamed piercingly and let it fall on the table as though it had burnt a hole in her palm. She herself refused to have her fortune told, shaking her head violently and flapping her arms in the air at the suggestion. Hadn't she suffered enough?

Bridget asked Mrs Prentice to deal the cards to Adolf. She looked at him enquiringly. He shrugged – there was no harm in it. The red cards predominantly spread before him denoted wealth and happiness. He would also know splendid health.

'Good, good,' he cried, inordinately pleased at this ridiculous prophecy. Often he had stomach cramps. Ever since the death of his mother he had been frightened of dying in pain. Not only would he have money but his path through life would be strewn with broken hearts. He himself wouldn't give a dickey bird. Tall nordic maidens, built like trees, would fall at his feet. They would die for him, blow their brains out for him.

When Bridget had passed on this extraordinary information, he glanced suspiciously at Mrs Prentice. She was obviously being sarcastic. He too had drawn the king of clubs, but it no longer signified a dark stranger. In his case the card stood for Alexander the Great. He was startled that she knew of such a name. Of all the kings in the pack, according to Mrs Prentice, he alone held the globe in his fingers.

Adolf said he must go upstairs. He had a fearful headache. To suggest he was tired wouldn't go down well with the women. He'd done very little. While they'd washed up he'd been crouched over the drain in the backyard.

He thanked Bridget and Mary O'Leary for the dinner and bowed stiffly in the direction of Mrs Prentice. He was outraged at the way she had continually referred to him as a portion of meat – either a sausage or a chicken leg or a lamb chop. It was a mercy, he thought, she lacked her teeth.

When he had climbed to the second floor and lain down on the couch, the room heaved up and down. He stretched his hand to the floor to steady himself. He thought of Meyer's son in an open boat, attempting to cover his men's boots with a woman's petticoat, hearing the Ragtime end and the strains of an Episcopal hymn floating out across the water as the *Titanic* dipped her bow.

He couldn't think how Alois could consume such quantities of alcohol and live.

22

Three days into the New Year, Adolf started work at the Adelphi Hotel. There being no vacancy in the sculleries or laundry rooms, he was given a pale grey uniform with a high collar edged in green braid and told to make himself useful in the main lounge and foyer. As the third under-manager was busy and the second under-manager spoke no German, Adolf's duties and obligations were explained to him by a Swiss pastry chef of advanced years. He could carry luggage, deliver telegrams, take orders for morning coffee and afternoon tea – but not for whisky sodas – and be sent into the town on discreet errands. He was warned that if he was caught using the front entrance of the hotel or seen spitting in the corridor he would immediately be dismissed and have his wages forfeited for the week concerned. If he was found stealing food from the kitchens he would be handed over to the police. At all times he must be clean and tidy and keep his fingernails ready for inspection. Had he understood? If it hadn't been for Alois and his predictable comments, Adolf was inclined to quit there and then. Haughtily he nodded his assent.

The instant he stepped through the pass-door into the body of the hotel, he was in his element. His feelings were those of the natural swimmer who, until that moment, hadn't known the exact location of the river. Sinking into the carpet of dusky pink that rolled a hundred feet across the marble floor, he floated between islands of small tables and elegant sofas to the foyer beyond. Apart from his beloved Opera House in Vienna, he had never seen so beautiful an interior. For once Alois had spoken the truth. Built to accommodate passengers in transit for the Atlantic run, the hotel itself with state rooms panelled in mahogany – Gymnasium and Café Parisien, Mary Pickford Saloon and companionways railed in shining brass – resembled a luxurious ocean liner. In the vast lounge hung with mirrors the Venetian chandeliers trembled as below stairs in the boiler room they stoked the furnaces night and day to raise steam in the Turkish bath.

No sooner had Adolf reached the flight of marble steps that led down into the foyer, than a gentleman making for the glass doors of the smoking room hailed him and pressing a coin into his hand told him to buy a certain newspaper. Inquiring of a page boy where he might find such an item, Adolf was pointed into the street and shown a kiosk below the level of the cab rank. Having purchased the newspaper, Adolf was about to run up the steps past the commissionaire when he remembered he must use the side door. Running, he climbed the hill, entered the tiled corridors and sprinting through what he took to be the pass-door found himself in the kitchens. In this hell-hole of noise and heat and preparation he frantically sought redirection. A youth in a soiled apron apathetically led him down a further maze of corridors. Hurtling at last through swing doors, Adolf emerged into the lounge, sped panting across the carpet and entered the smoking room. He was given a sixpenny tip for his pains and, on muttering his thanks to the generous gentleman who stood before him, was addressed in his mother tongue, heavily accented:

'My name is Monsieur Dupont. Play fair by me and I will not disappoint you. Each morning I require the same newspaper. I desire it to be delivered at precisely nine o'clock, when I shall be in the Mauve Breakfast Room. At four o'clock you will fetch the afternoon edition. At that hour I shall be either in my suite on the first floor, or in the lounge. I prefer my newspaper to be folded into three sections, like so.'

Nodding, though he had not cared for the word 'fetch', Adolf promised he would do his best.

'I like your style,' said M. Dupont who, in a grey morning suit and black silk tie, was every inch the gentleman.

'I believe myself to be a good judge of character. You're a man to rely on.'

Pale with gratitude, his face tinted blue and gold from the reflection of the stained-glass windows, Adolf left the smoking room and hung about the foyer. He was annoyed with himself for having been so eager to oblige, running like a rabbit up hill and down dale; and yet in his hand he held the rewards of such servility. His mind boggled at the thought of the money he might earn if he fetched regularly for M. Dupont. At the end of the week he would hand over every penny of his tips and wages to Alois; he couldn't wait to see the astonishment on his brother's supercilious face. With this first sixpence, however, he resolved to buy Pat a small clockwork train.

As it happened, when Adolf arrived at the kiosk at five to four he realised he must use a portion of the sixpence if he was to purchase the newspaper at all. Upon return-ing to the hotel and arriving in the lounge gasping for breath, he found M. Dupont seated at a round table enjoying a pot of tea and a dish of muffins.

M. Dupont took the folded newspaper, thanked him, and reminded him of the need for punctuality.

'Nine o'clock, sharp,' he repeated. 'Not a second before or later.'

Annoyed that M. Dupont, despite his earlier claims, had proved to be a disappointment, and ashamed to loiter lest it should seem he was begging, Adolf walked away.

In the evening, when Alois asked him if he had received any gratuities, he replied huffily that as he supposed he was to be paid wages for the work he was doing he didn't expect to be given tips. Indeed he would refuse them, if offered.

The following morning at nine he again paid for M. Dupont's newspaper. In return M. Dupont thanked him.

By mid-afternoon Adolf was thoroughly annoyed with himself. He wondered if he should seek the advice of the head porter.

He had just made up his mind to confront M. Dupont and ask him outright for the penny-halfpenny needed to purchase the afternoon edition, when M. Dupont appeared on the steps of the foyer and beckoned him. Drawing him to one side, he slipped a shilling into his hand and a large key.

'Go to my suite,' he said. 'In the entrance hall you will see a brown paper parcel on a chair. Take the parcel to No. 89, Pitt Street and ask for Mr Brackenberry. Deliver it personally into Mr Brackenberry's hands. Then return the key to me. I shall be in the Turkish bath.'

'And the newspaper?' said Adolf. 'Shall I also bring the newspaper?'

'No,' M. Dupont said. 'I won't need the newspaper today.'

Pitt Street, Adolf found, was in the Chinese quarter of the city, below the unfinished cathedral. No. 89 was a Chinese provision store situated next door to a laundry. Thinking there was perhaps some mistake, he walked up and down outside for several minutes, watched by four Lascar seamen who sat barefooted on the steps of the house opposite. Clutching his parcel he entered the shop and retreated instantly, overcome by the smell of dried fish. An elderly Chinaman stared down at him inscrutably from a first-floor window.

'Herr Brackenberry,' called Adolf nasally, holding his hand over his nostrils.

The Chinaman withdrew and closed the window.

Nonplussed, Adolf was about to return to the hotel when a stout man with a cut over one eye came out of the store.

'Brackenberry,' he announced abruptly.

Adolf held out the parcel.

'Know anything?' said the man, not taking it.

Adolf stared at him.

'Righty-ho,' cried the stout man and making up his mind he snatched the parcel from Adolf's hand and doubled back inside the store.

The Lascar seamen rose from the steps, humming like mosquitoes.

As Adolf walked away from No. 89 he was aware of the little brown men padding along the pavement in pursuit. Only when he had turned into the genteel respectability of Rodney Street did they cease to follow him. Glancing nervously over his shoulder he watched them standing in a row, no bigger than children, watching his departure.

M. Dupont was lying half-naked on an Egyptian couch inlaid with brass. Groaning, he asked Adolf what Brackenberry had looked like.

'Battered,' said Adolf. 'His brow was slashed by a knife.'

'Mon Dieu!' cried M. Dupont, starting up from the couch in alarm. Sweat oozed from the folds of his belly.

Hastily Adolf assured him it was an old wound.

'How tall?' demanded M. Dupont, impatiently.

Adolf described a large man of some weight, wearing a checked motoring coat.

'That's him,' said M. Dupont, relaxing. 'Did he say anything?'

'Nothing I understood,' confessed Adolf, and he laid the key to M. Dupont's suite on the mosaic floor of the Turkish bath.

'One shouldn't take too much notice of appearances,' remarked M. Dupont, closing his eyes. 'Things are never as they seem.'

'You don't have to tell me,' Adolf said. 'Only recently a dear friend of mine mentioned that his son, to all intents and purposes a man, was to be seen in a lifeboat dressed as a woman. The fact that Herr Brackenberry was living next door to a Chinese laundry doesn't make me necessarily conclude that he was a laundryman.'

'Who the devil are you?' asked M. Dupont, opening his eyes in alarm.

Adolf assured him he was a penniless student, forced by his stingy half-brother to seek employment.

'That's enough,' cried M. Dupont testily. 'I must be allowed to perspire in peace.'

23

Before sitting down to supper, Adolf presented Bridget with a threepenny bunch of violets.

Pleased, she placed them in a jam jar in the centre of the table.

Adolf hinted that if he were in charge of management at the hotel he would think of a more efficient system of serving light refreshments in the lounge. 'I have run miles,' he complained. 'From table to cash desk and back again. I'm allowed to serve tea and accept payment but I'm not authorised to carry loose change in my pocket. I have to dash the entire length of the room to prise the necessary coppers out of the cashier behind the swing doors.'

'You don't have to dash,' cried Alois, who wasn't due at the hotel until nine o'clock. 'There's no need to be dramatic.'

'Indeed I have to,' snapped Adolf. 'I have been told

that unless I hurry customers may leave the hotel either without paying or without signing the appropriate chit of paper.'

'You know nothing of the problems,' Alois said. 'Nothing at all. One day at the Ritz in Paris, every waiter with ten shillings' worth of change in his purse made as one man for the exit and was never seen again.'

'My point exactly,' shouted Adolf. 'Only I am referring to the guests, not the waiters. Under the present system, my work is time-consuming and exhausting. I'm continually on the trot.'

Bridget, seeing that Alois was growing red in the face with indignation, remarked that it was obvious that Adolf was a success at the hotel. She looked admiringly at the violets.

'Moderately, yes,' agreed Adolf. 'I have been in a position to do someone a small favour.' He explained how M. Dupont had given him his key and how he had gone to the first floor suite and collected a parcel which he had later delivered to luxurious business premises somewhere in the region of the Cotton Exchange.

'Didn't they tell you the rules?' demanded Alois. 'You aren't allowed inside the rooms. What was the fellow's name?'

Adolf refused to give him any more information. Alois should mind his own business. He had been told he might be sent on discreet errands. It would be far from discreet to divulge the name of the guest concerned.

'You'll be seen,' threatened Alois. 'And reported. There are house detectives permanently on duty in the corridors.'

Adolf said he had seen no one in the corridors and in any case, as long as he refrained from spitting, he had nothing to fear.

'You're a bloody fool,' shouted Alois. 'You are wet behind the ears.'

24

For the rest of the week Adolf continued to buy M. Dupont his newspaper, morning and afternoon. Some days he was neither paid nor tipped, on others he received a shilling. As his rate of tipping had increased, he felt he was breaking even.

On the Friday he was again approached by M. Dupont and given the key to the upstairs suite. Again he delivered a brown paper parcel, somewhat larger and rattling as he carried it, to the scarred Mr Brackenberry in Pitt Street.

This time, upon returning to the Turkish bath, he was urged to take a florin from the pocket of M. Dupont's towelling robe. He was tempted to grovel on the wet tiles out of gratitude.

His working day, which began at six-thirty in the morning and ended at five-thirty in the evening, was further prolonged on the Saturday when he was ordered by the under-manager to stay until midnight. Two waiters were off sick and a third had been taken into custody the previous day for secreting a chicken in aspic under his bowler hat. Though tired, Adolf was glad to oblige, for it meant he would be in the hotel at the same time as Meyer.

He hadn't realised that he would also be working with Alois. It irritated and offended him to watch his brother, a napkin over one arm, deferentially emptying ash trays into a paper bag.

'Go away,' cried Alois, seeing Adolf in the doorway of the smoking room. 'You have no right in here.'

'I go where I please,' retorted Adolf. 'I'm not bolted to the floor.'

However, he left almost at once, not liking to observe his brother performing such a degrading task. It gave him no pleasure to think that old man Hitler, who at Alois's present age had been rising fast in the civil service, would turn in his grave to know that his eldest son was a part-time salesman of razor blades and a cleaner of ashtrays. It's different for me, thought Adolf: I know where I'm going – though at that moment he was merely carrying a plate of ham sandwiches towards a party of naval gentlemen seated in the far corner of the lounge.

He was further disillusioned later in the evening when, having been sent into the Lilac Supper Room to deliver a cablegram, he saw Meyer on a raised dais, wearing a paper hat and accompanying on his violin a young woman who, dressed as if for sun-bathing, was singing a song about a policeman.

He fled, unable to be a witness to Meyer's shame.

At midnight he fully intended to avoid both Alois and Meyer and go home alone; but at eleven o'clock Alois came into the foyer and said that Meyer wanted to see him urgently. Would he go to B Corridor, below stairs, immediately?

Mystified, Adolf did as instructed. He found Meyer, still sporting his paper hat, walking up and down in some agitation.

'I must explain,' Meyer said, and paused.

'There's no need,' Adolf told him gently. 'A man must work. Who am I to pass judgment? You mustn't be at a loss for words.'

Puzzled, Meyer stared at him. He said he thought Adolf had misunderstood his meaning. The matter was a delicate one. But for a certain happening, he would never have involved him – as things stood he had no choice. Certain persons, whom he couldn't name, had for some while been involved in a certain type of activity. There was no time to go into details. Sufficient to say that it was socially important work, with political undertones. 'I must stress,' said Meyer, 'the need for courage. The work is dangerous. It's only fair I should tell you this.'

'I'm not afraid,' asserted Adolf, though his heart was beginning to thump in his breast.

Placing an approving hand on the young man's sleeve,

Meyer continued. 'Tonight I received information regarding certain events that may take place within the next two hours. I cannot leave here until twelve-thirty at the latest. A message must be delivered before then to a certain person. You yourself, after a week's training running backwards and forwards across the lounge, are the one person capable of carrying a message at speed. Will you do it?'

Flustered, Adolf asked: 'This certain person – will he be in a certain place?'

'In the basement of our house,' revealed Meyer. 'It is none other than Mary O'Leary. Tell her to go to the doctor's house and arrange for drinks all round.'

'Drinks all round,' repeated Adolf. He was beginning to suspect that Meyer had already been drinking.

'Mary O'Leary will understand what I mean. Will you do it?'

'I cannot refuse,' said Adolf. 'Though after a hard day's work I do feel—'

'Rest assured,' Meyer interrupted gravely, nodding his head in its paper hat, 'that what you are doing is of the utmost importance. You are furthering a just and noble cause, young Adolf. And not a word to Alois.'

Two minutes before midnight, the ends of his trousers tucked into the tops of his threadbare socks, Adolf slipped out of the side door of the hotel. Keeping his elbows close to his ribs and breathing rhythmically, he began to run strongly up Brownlow Hill.

170

25

After conveying his message to Mary O'Leary, Adolf was
all for going upstairs and falling asleep. He had been on
his feet, and running on them at that, for almost eighteen hours. Mary O'Leary, judging by the mottled
complexion of her face and neck, had been sitting dozing
by the fire for most of the day. 'You're needed,' she said
firmly. 'You're too fond of lying down. Come along.'

Protesting, Adolf followed her up the area steps into
the street. He couldn't think what sort of important social
work Mary O'Leary could possibly be involved in. He
had attended many meetings in Vienna, of various political persuasions, and had never come across anyone
remotely resembling this mountain of a woman, dressed
in rags, the backs of her hands so covered in black hair
that they seemed to be encased in mittens.

'Let me take your arm,' she said. 'Support me. We will
look less conspicuous.' It being now one hour into Sunday

171

morning and a day of rest ahead, there were still people in the streets, many of them walking the worse for drink or hanging on to railings, too confused to advance further.

When they reached the doctor's house, they found the front door already open. Peering anxiously into the road was a youth with crinkly black hair. Sighting Mary O'Leary, he jumped up and down and shouted: 'He's inside, Missus.'

Mary O'Leary marched past him and down the hall without a word. Propped against the wall was a rusty bicycle.

Upon entering the back room they were greeted not by Kephalus but by the man Adolf had surprised leaping through the wall in Stanhope Street. Though his head was no longer bandaged he wore on his feet those unmistakable golfing shoes first seen in Meyer's wardrobe. Set on the table in front of the window Adolf was disgusted to see the plate of custard tarts offered to him, more than a month ago, by the doctor.

'You've heard,' said Mary O'Leary.

'Yes,' the man said. 'Is it drinks all round?'

'The sooner the better.'

'I'll be off on the bike. You sit here until I send word.' The man left the room at once and was heard calling to the boy at the door to take the bicycle down the steps.

'I'll say goodnight,' said Adolf.

'You'll stay where you are,' ordered Mary O'Leary.

'There's work to be done before long.' She inspected the cakes on the table. Finding them too far gone to be eatable, she shrugged and standing on the tips of her massive boots reached up to adjust the working lamp that hung from the ceiling.

Adolf sat on the floor in near darkness. Tired as he was he couldn't sleep. He wondered what Meyer had meant by danger. Was it imminent or to come later? Would he be set upon by thugs or shot at from a distance? He devoutly hoped the front door was securely bolted.

'What are we to expect?' he demanded at last. 'Who are we waiting for?'

'The night men are coming,' said Mary O'Leary, perched on a beer crate beside the hearth. This sentence, once understood, struck Adolf as sinister in the extreme. His eyes widened in alarm.

'I haven't the words,' said Mary O'Leary. 'Meyer will explain later.'

An hour passed. Mice could be heard squeaking behind the skirting board. Then footsteps sounded in the hall and the curly-headed boy burst into the room.

'Argyll Street,' he shouted. 'Off Scottie Road.' Speaking directly to Adolf, he asked: 'Are youse the foreign fella?'

'He is,' said Mary O'Leary, bustling to the door.

'Meyer says he's to come with you, Missus,' the boy told her.

Stumbling down the steps, Adolf thankfully left the doctor's house. He had no idea where they were going, but he thought he stood more chance of survival in the open.

Once into the road, the boy disappeared. Beyond the black pit of St James's cemetery, the lights of ships anchored in the river swung up and down against the sky.

Mary O'Leary led Adolf back along the streets he had so strenuously run through earlier that night. Even at this hour the windows of the Adelphi Hotel blazed like beacons – the revolving doors still spun. They travelled the length of Lime Street and up the steep incline of London Road. Argyll Street was situated to the north of Scotland Road, an area of the city so wretched and notorious that Adolf was glad to be accompanied by Mary O'Leary. He had the feeling their progress was being closely watched. It seemed to him that they were both preceded and followed by a dark figure who from time to time darted away down side streets only to reappear either further ahead of them or some way behind. And yet this person, or persons, kept their distance.

Though Adolf sighed heavily on occasions, signifying his exasperation at being expected to traipse about the town in the middle of the night, he felt curiously elated. No one, as far as he could remember, since he was sixteen years old had needed or asked for his assistance. He had always been shy and introverted, more so after the death of his mother and the death of his hopes, when they had deliberately barred him from the Art Academy. People hadn't often told him jokes or sent him postcards when they went on holiday. Secretly he thought it was because he was disliked. Of course Meyer had intimated he had no choice – it was inconceivable to think of Alois in his homburg hat jogging hot-foot on such a mysterious errand – but perhaps Meyer had truly seen through the cold exterior to the warm heart within. It was a queer feeling to be trusted.

Mary O'Leary was guiding him down a narrow street of workmen's cottages. It was unnaturally quiet. Despite the thin drizzle that had begun to fall, a stench of garbage and something worse rose from the muddy ground. Not a soul was about and only one solitary lamp burned at the end of the street. Adolf had heard stories of the fearful happenings in this sector of the city – the drunkenness, the fights, the suicidal women who ruptured their wombs with the tip of a broken bottle. There wasn't a single inhabitant, according to Alois, who wasn't destined for the workhouse, the prison or the Infirmary. The police, if present at all, patrolled in groups of three.

Suddenly Mary O'Leary said urgently: 'Hold fast to my arm and tilt your face to the lamp.'

Adolf didn't understand her. As he hesitated, standing there in the middle of the gloomy street, he was encircled by shadowy figures and torn abruptly from her side. Jostled and manhandled, numerous fingers clawing at his throat, he was pushed against a wall.

'Leave him,' he heard Mary O'Leary cry. 'He brought the message. Leave him be.'

Her words were repeated by a dozen voices . . . He brought the message . . . He's the fella that brought the message . . . and then he was being supported on either side, a hand under each elbow, and run down the street at such speed that his ankles knocked together. Finally he was lifted from the ground and borne, coat ends flapping and head jiggling violently on the stem of his neck, around a corner and into a cobbled court. Narrowly escaping decapitation, he was carried through the doorway of a house and dropped on his feet. He faced a broken table, shorn up at one end by a pile of bricks, behind which Meyer sat, writing on a piece of paper by the light of a candle.

'Excellent,' cried Meyer at the sight of him. 'Good work, young Adolf.'

When his eyes had grown accustomed to the dim light, Adolf made out Kephalus standing in a corner of the room, clutching a torch and a Gladstone bag presumably containing medical supplies. Beneath a sink under the window huddled several women, holding children in their arms. Meyer seemed to be giving detailed instructions to the half-dozen men who had escorted Adolf to

176

the house. At his elbow rolled a shillelagh. When the men trooped out of the door, the candle flickered in the draught.

'There's little time for talking,' said Meyer addressing Adolf, who leaned more dead than alive against the sink. 'The night men are coming. Go up on to the roof and keep watch. Kephalus will explain what is expected of you.'

Pointing his torch downwards, the doctor preceded Adolf up a flight of stairs that threatened to collapse under their weight. On a torn mattress on the floor lay a row of children, turned on their sides and all packed the same way like sardines in a box. Flashing his torch upwards, exposing a ceiling that in places was open to the elements, Kephalus ordered Adolf to climb on his shoulders and push up the skylight.

'I haven't the strength,' complained Adolf. 'I'm not a mountaineer.'

Ignoring his protests, the doctor squatted on his haunches and jabbed him in the shins with the torch. Adolf scrambled on to Kephalus' back, gritting his teeth, and held tight to his ears. Rising together in an unsteady pyramid, they swayed back and forth searching for the trap door.

Moments later, one elbow badly scraped, Adolf levered himself through the aperture and lifting the Gladstone bag and torch after him emerged on to the roof. Clinging to the chimney breast, he saw in the distance the lamps of Scotland Road and beyond, luminous against the dark clouds, the glittering rectangle of the Adelphi Hotel.

Kephalus leaped for the edge of the trap door and athletically hauled himself upwards by the strength of his arms. Coughing and wheezing he wriggled his way on to the broken tiles and rolled towards the guttering.

'Stay in one place,' pleaded Adolf. 'The roof will come down.' Fleetingly he remembered, clinging there in the rain, how as a boy of eighteen he had prayed for a second Boer War. He had felt that until his life was blown sky-high by some monstrous explosion and fell earthwards in differently arranged pieces he would never, ever find himself.

'Move over,' ordered Kephalus. 'You look north and I'll look south. Keep your ears open.'

'For what?' asked Adolf crossly, unable to let go of the chimney stack.

'Footsteps,' said Kephalus. 'Movements. When the call comes, drop through the trap door like a shooting star and shout to Meyer beneath. Then hand the children up to me.'

He began to prowl about the chimney, slithering on all fours in the darkness. A tile bounced from the roof and fell into the court below. 'Take care,' called a voice, and the beam of a torch flashed for a moment some-where to the right.

'At this rate,' whispered Adolf, 'I won't have to wait till the call comes. Nor will I need to use the trap door.' He could make no sense of it. He couldn't understand why the children were required to be lifted on to the roof. Was he about to witness some massacre of the innocents? He waited at least ten minutes before intimating to Kephalus that if it was all the same to him he preferred to go indoors.

'I've been working since six o'clock this morning,' he explained. 'And my constitution is far from robust. I'm a martyr to bronchitis.'

'Keep your voice low, you little twerp,' hissed Kephalus.

The word, though unfamiliar to Adolf, wasn't, he thought, an endearment. He slid downwards until his buttocks rested upon the tiles and his feet sloped towards the guttering. If he was quiet and made no trouble, perhaps the doctor would cease his perilous meanderings about the stack. It was possible, Adolf hoped, to fall twenty feet and live. Somewhere behind him a match was struck; he caught the faint drift of tobacco smoke.

'Listen,' whispered Kephalus. 'It may be that in most cases it is better for the children to be taken into the care of the authorities. They get rid of the lice and they cut them out of their undergarments. But emotionally it is disruptive and cruel. Do you agree?'

'I do, I do,' said Adolf.

'It's not overcrowding in the bed that causes contagious

179

diseases – it's the state of the drains and the Catholic Church and the rats coming through the woodwork. It's the lack of food. How do they expect a man to provide adequate nourishment for his wife and himself, let alone fourteen children?'

'He could work harder,' suggested Adolf, recklessly.

'Work harder!' cried the doctor. His voice from behind the chimney rose in outrage. 'What is that supposed to mean? By my information, until this week you've spent the greater proportion of your time flat on your back. Do you know that at the gates of the docks at five o'clock every morning they fight like animals for the privilege of working for three shillings a day?'

'I spoke without thinking,' said Adolf hastily. 'I'm ashamed.' He was desperately afraid the doctor meant to leap on him and dash him to the cobbles below. He said again, and with as much feeling as he could muster: 'I spoke without thinking.'

A child whimpered in the room beneath. The doctor grunted and fell silent.

26

Two figures appeared at the far end of the street holding storm lanterns. They stood motionless on the corner, giving no sign that they intended to approach further. From somewhere at roof level Adolf heard the incongruous ringing of a bicycle bell.

When the call came, seconds later, it was surprisingly muted, a low wailing that hardly rose above a murmur. Adolf, who had expected to hear a pistol shot or the thrilling blast of a trumpet, strained his ears to catch its drift. They are coming . . . The night men are coming . . .

'Quick,' urged the doctor, but already Adolf was clinging upright to the stack, only too eager to leave his precarious post. Judging by the commotion from the downstairs room, the scuffle of boots and muffled cursing, he had no need to warn Meyer. He had just managed to turn about and was lowering himself feet first through the trap-door when a hand gripped him by the hair.

'Too late,' cried Kephalus. 'The bastards have come from both directions.'

Hauling Adolf skywyards again, he kicked the trap into place and forcing Adolf to lean at an acute angle against the roof flung a weighty arm across his shoulders. They lay cheek to cheek on the wet tiles. On his re-entry through the sky-light Adolf had struck his forehead on the corner bricks of the crumbling chimney stack. He couldn't be sure if the moisture beneath his face was rain or blood. The flimsy guttering beneath the toe-caps of his boots was all that stopped him from sliding earthwards, locked in a comradely embrace with the doctor.

It was impossible to see what was happening in the little court, but now the sounds of the battle were clearly audible – doors slamming, children crying, tables being overturned.

Then voices were heard directly beneath them and Meyer's voice raised louder than all the rest. 'God damn you,' he was shouting over and over. 'God damn you to hell.'

By moving himself fractionally from the doctor's side and tucking in his chin, Adolf was able to peer, through a gap in the leaking roof, into the room below. The scene he witnessed was so melodramatic in content and so jerkily enacted, that he felt he was watching a show at a moving picture house. Against the wall were ranged four or five women, each clutching a child to her breast. Facing

182

them and holding a lantern at shoulder height was a burly man in a raincoat. Between the trembling women and their persecutor stood Meyer in an heroic pose, brandishing his shillelagh. There were other persons in the room but they were merely onlookers. The man in the raincoat was deliberating upon which child he should snatch from its mother. Meyer was waiting to strike him dead if he took a step forward. At that instant a boy some two years old, clinging to his mother's neck, uttered a piercing shriek of terror. Adolf remembered suddenly a day in summer when in a field he had watched a dog chasing a dozen rabbits up a grassy slope. There had been no reason to suppose that the dog would be swift enough to catch any of them. And then one rabbit out of all the rest, as if sensing it had been chosen for death, froze in its tracks and screamed. Pouncing, the dog was on it and breaking its back in the grass.

Meyer, caught off balance by the piteous cry behind him, wavered in intention. The man in the raincoat held out his hand authoritatively. Passively the woman delivered up the child. Carrying the boy under one arm, the man with the lantern made for the stairs. The room was plunged into darkness.

Raising his head, Adolf saw it was almost dawn. He gripped the edge of the stack and pulled himself to his knees. Above the river wisps of scarlet cloud trailed across a strip of dark blue sky. Below him a procession of children, some holding babies in their arms, accompanied by five or six officials at the most, were being herded towards a black Maria parked at the corner of Scotland Road. In every doorway along the length of the street stood men and women, perfectly silent, watching the children go.

Descending into the house, Adolf and the doctor found Meyer seated at the broken table in an attitude of dejection. He looked up as Kephalus approached and raised his hands in despair.

'Ai, ai,' he wailed.

'We saved a few,' comforted the doctor. 'Next time it will be more.' He patted Meyer clumsily on the shoulder.

'Who were they?' asked Adolf. 'The men with the lanterns?'

'Civil servants,' answered Kephalus. 'Men from the City Corporation.'

'I don't understand,' said Adolf. 'There were hundreds of you and not a dozen of them. They didn't even use the police.'

'Let the minority act with enough authority,' cried Meyer bitterly, 'and the majority will walk like lambs to the slaughter.'

He told Adolf it would be more prudent if he went home alone. It would do him no good to be seen in this vicinity with either the doctor or himself. The boy he had met earlier at Kephalus' house would see him safely to Stanhope Street.

'Wear this,' said the doctor, thrusting a cap into Adolf's hands. 'You want to hide that cut on your brow. Ask Mary O'Leary to bathe it with salt and water.'

The youth with curly hair escorted Adolf through the back streets of the town, indicating by signs and gestures that it was too dangerous to use the main thoroughfares. Arriving by a devious route at the bottom of St James Road, he led Adolf to the gates of the cemetery.

Adolf stood his ground. The boy urged him forward.

'No,' said Adolf. He was exhausted enough as it was, without stumbling along the winding paths of the grave-yard.

The boy pointed across the cemetery towards the cata-combs and the steep wall of granite that rose to street level. He mimed the climbing of a cliff.

'Out of the question,' snapped Adolf.

He strode purposefully away around the curve of the railings and began to ascend the hill towards Hope Street.

After a moment's hesitation, the boy followed. Crossing to the opposite side of the road and glancing nervously at Adolf, he walked abreast of him up the hill.

Such precautions, thought Adolf, were absurd. Meyer had delusions of grandeur. He had spoken as if he were plotting a revolution, and all he had done was to posi-tion a few men on a few roof-tops and ring a bicycle bell.

It wasn't only the wretched inhabitants of Argyll Street who had been cowered into submission by a handful of men acting with authority – Meyer too had bleated like a sheep at the first scent of the wolf.

He had turned wearily into lower Stanhope Street, the boy still keeping pace with him though still on the other side of the road, when he saw several policemen approaching from the opposite direction. He faltered and looked across at the boy, who had stopped and was clearly judging the distance between himself and the advancing constables. Making up his mind, the boy shouted something to Adolf and began to run towards them.

Adolf was convinced the boy was making a futile effort to reach the safety of Mary O'Leary's basement. He too began to run desperately in the same direction, though he had no such conviction. He argued to himself that one could hardly be arrested for running at a policeman. If he failed to reach the basement in time and they accosted him, he would denounce the boy and say he was chasing him because he was a pick-pocket. Panting, various fantasies rushing through his mind, the blue uniforms looming closer, he pursued the youth and was startled to find that he had swerved down an alleyway and they were no longer on a collision course with the forces of law and order.

'Hurry, hurry,' shouted the boy, who had now stopped at the base of a stunted tree that grew beside a brick wall. Urging Adolf to climb on to a withered branch, he pushed and heaved him aloft.

Stubbornly Adolf clung to the tree and refused to go further. He hadn't an ounce of strength left in his body. The blast of a policeman's whistle sounded from beyond the alleyway. Springing for the wall, he scrambled over the top and dropped into a back-yard. The boy landed lightly as a cat beside him and, dragging him by brute force towards a door, opened it and thrust him inside.

There, sitting astride his bicycle in a dimly lit passage, was the man in golfing shoes, and beyond him, his hand on the rail of the stairs, waited Meyer. A tremendous hammering began on the front door.

'Take him upstairs,' said Meyer to the man on the bicycle.

'It's no use,' protested Adolf. 'I prefer to give myself up. I have done no wrong.'

'Your papers are not in order,' said Meyer curtly. 'Go with Michael Murphy and he will show you how easy it is to reach home safely. Remember only to close the door behind you. You will be in your bed before five minutes is up, I promise you.'

Michael Murphy ran ahead of Adolf up the stairs. On the second landing they passed a woman of frightening pallor sitting on a deck chair nursing a coal-black baby. The woman nodded and wished them good morning. She seemed oblivious both of their villainous appearance and of the noise issuing from the hall below. The English, thought Adolf, are a nation of eccentrics and fearfully dangerous. No wonder they ruled an empire.

Reaching the third floor, Michael Murphy opened a door at the end of the passage. The room faced on to the dance hall opposite.

'I'm not climbing along window-ledges,' cried Adolf passionately.

The next moment Michael Murphy laid violent hands upon him. He was turned to the wall and hurled towards it. He lifted up his arms to shield his face. There was a sound of paper ripping and then he was lying across the mattress in Meyer's top room.

Remembering to close the door after him, he crept down the stairs to the second floor. Without bothering to remove his cap or his coat he flung himself on to the couch and fell instantly asleep.

27

Bridget decided to take the baby to the park on Sunday afternoon for an airing. Hearing the pram bumping down the steps, Mary O'Leary poked her head round the basement door and asked: 'Are you going to visit your cousin?'

'I'm away to look at the ducks. I'll go out of my mind if I stay cooped up there much longer.'

'I'll walk with you,' said Mary O'Leary. 'There's someone I have to see.' She hadn't a dinner to prepare. Not today. Meyer was off his food.

Bridget walked up and down the pavement while Mary O'Leary stoked the fire. Across the road a well-dressed man had stopped to read a notice attached to the railings of the church.

'The more I think about it,' said Bridget, as they walked up the Boulevard against a bitterly blowing wind, 'the more I'm inclined to swallow my pride. I've nothing to lose.' She was talking as usual about writing to her mother in Ireland and suggesting that bygones be bygones.

Mary O'Leary, who had taken part in this conversation many times before and never tired of it, agreed she hadn't. It seemed to her a miraculous thing to have a mother, even one not on speaking terms.

'I've darling Pat to consider,' said Bridget. 'Alois isn't a man to rely on. He studies young Adolf more than me. I never saw a penny of Adolf's wages yesterday and by the look of him this morning he lost the lot during the night.'

'He was out gambling, was he?' asked Mary O'Leary.

'He was out somewhere, that's for sure. You should see the state of him. I'd counted on putting a few coppers aside for a rainy day. Alois could be off into the blue tomorrow and then what would I do?'

'Suffer and wait,' said Mary O'Leary. 'That's all we're good for.'

They crossed the road and went through the ornamental gates into the park. It was too cold for crowds.

'I should have kept on with me singing lessons,' fretted Bridget, gazing discontentedly at the brutally pruned rose bushes spaced at intervals along the borders of the gravel path. 'When I was sixteen a gentleman in Dublin said I had perfect pitch.' She felt she'd been cut back in her prime and would never flower again.

'I was good with the needle,' recollected Mary O'Leary. 'As a girl. I could have gone for a milliner.'

'You told me,' said Bridget, and she tried not to look

at the destroyed ribbons swinging from the remnants of Mary O'Leary's bonnet.

They discussed Mrs Prentice's Elsie and a woman who'd been caught putting a sliver of glass in her husband's scouse and whether Dr Kephalus had a woman or not. It would be like keeping company with an ash-tray. Mary O'Leary had once observed him going into that shop in Brownlow Hill, the one selling books wrapped in brown paper covers. Bridget said she had no doubt Alois was a regular customer at the same counter. They were all brutes. Neither of them mentioned Meyer in this connection.

When they had walked twice around the railings of the pond, Mary O'Leary said she'd be off. She preferred streets to parks. It made her feel lonely with only pieces of grass and bits of trees to look at.

When she had gone Bridget sat down on a wooden bench and with a twig poked back the wodge of news-paper that had worked free from the gaping sole of her boot. Several boys ran past, rolling old bicycle wheels along the path. Approaching her from the other side of the pond, and cutting directly across the grass, was a tall gentleman comfortably clothed against the weather. When he was only a few yards from her she thought it was the same man she had seen outside the church.

Tipping his hat to her, he asked: 'Have you by any chance seen a lady in a brown fur coat pass this way?'

'I've not,' said Bridget. 'But then I've not been look-ing.' She wasn't a fool. She looked across the expanse of park. There wasn't anybody in sight. 'I'm a respectable married woman,' she said, and rising she let the brake off the pram.

'Let me take you into my confidence,' said the man hurriedly, and he removed his hat altogether and stood there, twirling it round and round by the brim. 'I have reason to believe we have mutual friends. I am anxious to get in touch with them. Would I be right in saying your husband is a man with exceptionally blue eyes?'

Bridget wasn't sure what to do for the best. He looked a gentleman, but then one could never tell. She thought she detected the faintest hint of brogue in his speech. Alois was always so secretive. He said he was out selling his old razors but he could be up to anything. She didn't want to land him in trouble. She began to walk away, pulling the pram behind her.

'Wait,' called the man. 'Please.'

He wasn't a bad-looking fellow. He had blue eyes himself and a well-trimmed beard.

'The person I'm referring to,' he said, 'is a devoted husband and son. I have seen him going into a certain hotel in the town. I'm very anxious to contact him.'

'Well, I can't help you,' said Bridget. 'My husband is six-foot tall, dark as the ace of spades and he doesn't like me talking to strangers.'

Swinging the pram round she wheeled it rapidly towards the gates. When she looked back over her shoulder the man hadn't moved.

28

Adolf slept for fifteen hours and woke to find himself on the floor behind the sofa. Rising, he surprised Alois and Bridget at their supper.

'He's returned to the land of the living,' cried Alois, without bitterness.

Adolf thought Meyer must have had a word with him.

When he saw his reflection in the upstairs mirror it was apparent that for once Alois had behaved sensibly in removing him from the couch to the floor. His coat was torn at the elbow and hem and covered in a mixture of soot and dust, as were his hands and face. He wouldn't have looked out of place down a coal mine. Worse, he discovered a score of insect bites that extended over his chest and arms. When he had scrubbed himself clean he carried his coat and shirt downstairs and dropped them on the landing beside the aspidistra. Later he would take them into the back yard and flap them about in the air.

'Don't tell me you've lost your shirt?' said Bridget, seeing the bare throat beneath his jacket.

'I need a pair of scissors,' he said. 'I'm unable to take off this hat.'

Bridget was amused at having to cut the cap from his head. She stopped smiling when she saw the reason for it.

'Whatever was Mr Meyer thinking of?' she scolded.

Fetching a bowl of warm water she added a dash of vinegar and with a scrap of cloth began to sponge the congealed blood from his forehead.

'You certainly had a night on the town,' said Alois admiringly. 'It must have been hard work to keep pace with you.'

Adolf scratched himself and said nothing. The cut wasn't deep, but he had a lump the size of a half-crown above his left eyebrow.

'You best wash your hair,' Bridget told him. 'You smell like a chimney sweep.'

Adolf asked if he could have a word with Alois in private. Grinning, Alois followed him on to the landing. When shown the insect bites he smiled more broadly than ever.

'Next time,' he said, 'you want to be more careful which little lady's bed you step into.'

Nauseated by the implication, Adolf protested that he had spent the entire night on his feet. 'I need a bath in Lysol. And my clothes disinfected.'

'This isn't a Salvation Army hostel,' shouted Alois, growing annoyed.

Adolf went unhappily up the stairs to the bathroom. Taking off his trousers and jacket he attempted to open the door set with coloured glass. He was unsuccessful; it had been nailed into place. Contenting himself with the thought that if he had succeeded his trousers would undoubtedly have blown into the yard below, he shook his clothes over the ancient bath. Then he washed his hair and dressed again.

When he returned to the living room, Bridget sat him at the table and brought a comb through from the bedroom. Since his arrival in England his hair had grown.

'You can't go to work with that old lump showing,' she said. 'They'll think you're a fighting man.'

Parting his hair at the side she began gently to comb a section of it downwards so that it concealed the cut on his forehead.

'You may be wondering,' said Adolf, 'why I haven't given you my wages?'

'I did wonder, yes,' said Alois dryly.

'I've been thinking things over,' Adolf told him. 'You've been very generous with me, very patient. I'm not an easy person to live with.'

Alois looked at him suspiciously – he seemed to be sincere.

'I was telling the truth,' continued Adolf, 'when I said

196

Angela offered me the money you sent her. I didn't ask, believe me. You know Angela. She was never one for travelling, and as things stood it seemed the best way out. But now I think I ought to make a clean breast of it to the authorities.'

'I'd rather you didn't go into details,' said Alois hastily. 'It's none of my business, though I could give you a word of warning. Whenever I made a clean breast of things I found myself in jail. Perhaps in my case they were justified.'

'It takes two to make the bargain,' murmured Adolf.

'Quite so,' said Alois. 'I had hoped that after steady employment at the Adelphi you might want to come into the razor business.' He didn't believe what he was saying but felt it was expected of him. He was sure his brother, if engaged as a salesman, would either lose his box of samples or inadvertently slit a prospective buyer's throat.

'I don't think it would suit me,' said Adolf. 'But you see my difficulty. I had intended to give you every penny of my wages. But I'll need the money for the ticket, won't I?'

'What's he saying?' asked Bridget.

'He's not going to give us any money,' said Alois bluntly. It would serve no purpose to insist on Adolf's handing over a proportion of his wages for food. In the long run it would be cheaper to subsidise him. In his head he worked out that on Adolf's present rate of pay it would take several months for him to save the sum required.

197

'Why isn't he going to give you any money?' asked Bridget grimly. She flung the comb down on to the table.

'He's going back to Austria.'

'Ah,' said Bridget, trying hard to conceal her delight. 'And he's never even been to New Brighton.'

'I wasn't thinking of Austria,' Adolf said. 'I had in mind somewhere further off.' He didn't say how much further.

'Not go home?'

Alois looked at him in astonishment. It was one thing to scrape the money together for the fare to Linz, quite another to talk of distant regions of the earth. He was damned if he was going to let Adolf live at his expense if he was thinking in terms of South America.

'You forget,' Adolf told him. 'I have no home. Not since Mother died.' His eyes filled with water as he fought to restrain himself from scratching a spot on his neck. He had a bite under the ear that was crying out for attention.

'What the devil's up with you now?' asked Alois.

'I have my feelings,' said Adolf between clenched teeth.

'Sheer bloody sentimentality,' muttered Alois.

Bridget remarked that it was a pity Adolf was leaving so soon. She hoped she sounded regretful. Already she was thinking how much it would cost to buy a few yards of fabric to recover the couch. She'd burn the old one or make it into dusters.

'He'll probably be here for months,' remarked Alois bleakly. 'Possibly years.'

He had no time for Adolf at all – the man was inefficient, arrogant and as he said himself difficult to live with, blasted difficult. And yet there was something about the conversation that disturbed him. He didn't like it. He had married Bridget, fathered a child by her, and still he felt she was less familiar than Adolf. She belonged to the present and Adolf belonged to the past and at this moment the past seemed more real than either the present or the future.

'This delivering of parcels,' he asked irritably. 'For one of the guests. Is it regular?'

'Fairly regular,' said Adolf.

'And how much are you tipped each time?'

'Twopence,' lied Adolf. It was not that he deliberately sought to deceive Alois, but he wanted to buy himself a new pair of trousers as soon as possible. And a jacket. It was all right saving his wages towards his fare but maybe Alois would consider the tips as something different. He wasn't going to go without a new pair of trousers just because Alois wanted more money to put on the horses. For the next few weeks he resolved to fetch and carry for M. Dupont like a gun-dog. He would crawl on his belly if need be. It was unendurable to be wearing verminous clothes.

29

As it turned out, there wasn't a great deal of fetching to be done. Twice M. Dupont cancelled his afternoon newspaper. He was out most days or else busy upstairs. Several times Adolf loitered about the corridors of the first floor in the hope that M. Dupont would come upon him and remember some urgent errand. He was seen by a page-boy who warned him to be especially careful. Extra security men had been hired to patrol the building. Something was up. The disguises they got themselves into would take your breath away.

'He's one,' hissed the boy, pointing at a man in a leather coat who, a fraction before Adolf looked in that direction, had disappeared behind the life-sized statue of a marble god.

Though he had no doubt the boy was half-witted, Adolf could not help regarding with suspicion the stuffed bear that stood outside the entrance to the Sportsman's Bar.

If he had been employed night and day by the hotel he would have been perfectly happy, for there he wore his smart grey uniform and his undervest of laundered cotton with the monogram on the shoulder. But his work ended at half-past five. In the store room when he changed into his jacket and trousers he felt he became a leper; walking home through the crowded streets he imagined that the passers-by shrank from contact with him. He was forever sniffing his armpits or examining the seams of his coat. Alois complained that it was worse than living with a monkey. It began to affect Adolf's work. Once, spoken to in a hectoring manner by a stout Jewish gentleman who had ordered a glass of Russian tea and a dish of strawberries and cream, he was overcome by rage. The kitchen had dispatched him with the glass of tea and a jug of cream, but omitted the strawberries. 'Take the tray away,' ordered the gentleman. 'I wish the items to arrive simultaneously, not in dribs and drabs.' Purple in the face with supressed passion, Adolf picked up the tray and contrived to tip the contents of the cream jug into the gentleman's lap. And that's just for starters, he thought. Mollified he hastened to fetch a sponge and a basin of water.

Finally, unable to bear his condition any longer, Adolf turned to Meyer for help. Perhaps he would be loaned the dark blue jacket with the gold buttons. Since the fiasco of the revolution he had seen very little of him. He had expected to find him reduced and out of sorts and was surprised to see him seated cheerfully at the table in the front room, playing checkers with the doctor.

'Ah! the working man personified,' cried Kephalus at the sight of him.

'I will come back another time,' said Adolf, and he went out slamming the door violently behind him, hoping to bury the disgusting doctor under an avalanche of plaster.

The very next morning, having received his newspaper in the Mauve Breakfast Room, M. Dupont said: 'I have observed you going out by the front entrance and returning by the side entrance. Why is that, do you suppose?'

'Merely a rule,' explained Adolf. 'I have never questioned the logic.' Thankfully he pocketed a threepenny bit.

'By the way,' said M. Dupont. 'I would like you to run a little errand for me this afternoon. Meet me in the foyer at one o'clock sharp.'

'If it's all the same to you,' Adolf said carefully, 'it would be better if you yourself brought the parcel downstairs. We aren't allowed into the rooms.'

'How inconvenient,' sighed M. Dupont. 'Perhaps I should ask someone else.'

Adolf persuaded him that there was no need. If things went wrong, he told himself, he had both Meyer and Alois to speak for him. Meyer was highly thought of in the supper rooms.

At one o'clock when, trembling, he climbed the stairs to the first floor, he found the corridors completely deserted. Either the page boy had been exaggerating or else the house detectives were all drinking behind the closed doors of the linen room. Arriving safely in the foyer with the brown paper parcel under his arm, he was stopped by a man in a leather coat who said something incomprehensible to him. At that moment the head porter stepped forward and handing Adolf a prescription told him to go immediately to the chemists in Lord Street. The man in the leather jacket looked at the prescription, then at the head porter and dismissed Adolf with a wave of his hand.

It was raining outside. M. Dupont had impressed upon Adolf that it was vital to deliver the parcel to Mr Brackenberry by 1.45 at the latest. Adolf waited twenty minutes at the chemist for a bottle of cough mixture. When he returned to the hotel he positioned himself in the centre of the cab rank and whistled frantically for the commissionaire to come down the steps. The commissionaire told him forcefully to go round to the side door and do his own delivering. Adolf was forced to part with his threepenny bit.

He ran as fast as he could through the streets, but he was hampered by the raised umbrellas in every hand. He told himself it was just a manner of speech, M. Dupont's mania for punctuality.

Turning into Pitt Street he was alarmed to see a policeman hovering on the pavement in the vicinity of the Chinese provision store. He stopped and pretended to be looking into the window of an ironmonger's. A second policeman came out of the store, holding fast to the arm of a man who, by the loudness of his motoring coat, was instantly recognisable as Mr Brackenberry.

By now both Adolf and his paper parcel were saturated by the rain. He walked thoughtfully back to the hotel, pondering on how he would extricate himself from this dilemma in a dignified manner. It was obvious that he had been a fool. He no longer cared if he spent the rest of his days in his old coat and trousers. But for chance and the crowded chemists, he would now be locked in a cell at the Bridewell. The parcel in his arms was already sodden, and simply by pressing one finger to a portion of the wrapping he was able to split the paper.

He entered the hotel, made his way to the store room where he kept his outdoor clothes and, finding the place empty, examined the contents of the package. He wasn't surprised to uncover a quantity of silver spoons, snuff boxes, and various small articles of jewellery. Retying the parcel as best he could, he wrapped it in his outdoor coat and bundled it into a shoe cupboard. Then he went in search of M. Dupont. He wouldn't reproach that gentleman or even indicate that he knew what the parcel contained. He would merely tell him where it was hidden and how in future, though it was regrettable, he would have to fetch his own newspaper, morning and afternoon editions. Leaning forward through the steam of the Turkish bath he would drop the key to M. Dupont's suite into the damp folds of his belly.

M. Dupont was neither in the Turkish bath nor in the foyer. At four o'clock he failed to make an appearance in the lounge. Nobody had seen him since luncheon. On enquiring finally at the desk, Adolf was told that M. Dupont had paid his bill at 1.30 and left in a cab for New York, via Pier 47. I will drink a glass of water, thought Adolf, and think of something. I won't give way to panic.

There was only one sensible solution – all others could in the end point to his being an accessory – to return the parcel to the suite and leave the key in the lock. But how to get the parcel upstairs? After some thought Adolf purloined a tray from the kitchens and a white cloth. Returning to the store room he washed his hands and his perspiring face and carefully combed that lock of hair at a slant over his brow. Balancing on the palm of his hand what he hoped appeared to be a tray of afternoon tea, he crossed the Lounge. At this hour every sofa, every chair was occupied. On the dais a string quartet was playing a medley of waltzes by Strauss. Adolf could see himself reflected in the mirrors, dapper in his grey uniform, the edge of his tray glittering under the chandeliers as he threaded his way between the tables. The modernity and brilliance of the scene dazzled him. The air was filled with the buzz of voices, the tinkling of cups, the lilting strains of the violin. It seemed to him that the vast lounge had never been more beautiful. It was the best job he had ever had, even if it was his first. God damn M. Dupont to hell for this paradise lost. Tears in his eyes, he climbed the stairs to the first floor. Again he was lucky. There wasn't a soul in the corridors.

He had put his tray down momentarily on the green carpet and was fitting his key in the lock when a hand touched him on the shoulder. Turning, he looked full into the face of the bearded man who, that night in the square when he had fallen over the Christmas tree, had engineered his escape from the prostitute.

'Son,' said the bearded man, and would have said more only now Adolf, recovering from that second of paralysis, was running full tilt along the corridor having abandoned himself completely to some earlier ancestral condition when, chased by brontosauruses or demons and flooded with adrenalin, man had fled for the safety of the cave. Skidding around the curve of the staircase, he leapt into the foyer and hurled himself into the revolving doors. Emerging into the night air, he took the wall of the cab rank in his stride and landed on his feet in the street below. He felt immensely powerful as he sprinted along Lime Street and turned left towards the market. Minus his horse, he was Old Shatterhand himself, cunning as a coyote and determined to shake off his pursuers. Had there been a convenient rock in the middle of the city street he would have climbed to the top of it and pulling down the tram cables as though they were cobwebs shouted to the skies that he was great, he was glorious.

Then suddenly it was over – he had burnt himself out. Utterly spent, he dribbled to a standstill. He had to cling to a lamp-post in case he fell down on the pavement. I'm wearing the hotel uniform, he thought. I shall be charged with theft as well as being an accessory.

He had no idea how long he stood there, shuddering with fatigue, his teeth chattering in his head. He flapped back and forth like a rag as the pedestrains brushed past him. He was in a narrow street, his back to the lighted windows of a department store. Across the road was a warehouse of some kind with a small door at street level and a loading bay two storeys higher. Further down he could see a section of a cobbled square in which stood a circular urinal, open to the sky. Peering over the top of the ornamental grill, the lamplight clearly illuminating the plains of his face, was the man with the beard.

Adolf crossed the road and like an animal nosing for cover blundered through the door of the warehouse.

30

He was outside the Grand Salon of the Pondevedrian Embassy in Paris. Count Danilo was singing:

> 'I'm off to Chez Maxime
> To join the swirling stream
> For one brief hour enchanting . . .'

'Help me,' cried Adolf, and he fell into the arms of a young man who stood in the passageway beside a flight of stone steps.

> 'When people ask what bliss is
> I simply tell them, this is . . .'

'Steady on,' urged the young man, and he guided Adolf into a little cubbyhole set in the wall and assisted him on to a high stool.

'Where am I?' whispered Adolf. 'Is it possible I'm dead?'

'You're a queer colour,' the young man said, answering him in German, though in a tone of voice reminiscent of Mrs Prentice. 'But you're not yet a corpse.'

Several young women in low-cut dresses, cheeks heavily rouged and eyelashes dripping with lamp blacking, ran down the stairs.

'Look at this,' called the young man. 'Is he drunk or ill?'

The ladies took no notice. Smoothing their dresses and patting their curls into place, they swept through the pass-door on to the stage.

'You'll have to go,' the young man said. 'It's more than my job's worth. There are only artistes or scene shifters allowed through here and you're neither of those.'

'If I'm sent into the street,' protested Adolf, his voice stronger now, 'I shall be instantly taken into custody. There's a man waiting to pounce on me and drag me to the police station.'

'It's none of my concern,' muttered the young man, looking anxiously up and down the passageway. 'You shouldn't have misbehaved.'

'I didn't misbehave,' shouted Adolf. 'I swear it. It is too exhausting to go into the full details, concerning as they do a Chinese provision store and a matter of second-hand clothes and a French gentleman who duped me, but I'm telling the truth. I have committed no crime. I behaved foolishly, but only to save myself.' He paused fractionally. 'I didn't want to go under.'

'Ah!' murmured the young man.

Adolf waited. He gripped the edges of the stool as though he were in danger of drowning. He would only use Meyer's name as a last desperate measure. It was possible the young man hated his father.

31

At first Adolf strenuously resisted the suggestion, but eventually he realised he had no choice. As the young man so rightly stated, the theatre was a utility building – every cupboard, every inch of space had a purpose. Though it was against the rules, when the musicians were in the orchestra pit their sweethearts waited in the band room beneath the stage. Nor could Adolf be hidden in the Green Room, the Prop Room, the manager's office or the wardrobe. It was absurd to think he could pass unnoticed in the dressing rooms. If he did manage to squeeze himself behind the back drop, he would have to pray that the fly-man wasn't drunk. He could receive a fatal blow on the head from a carelessly dropped sand bag. Then there was the fireman who shone his torch into every corner of the building every half hour or so. 'And you'd be hiding for two of us,' concluded the young man. 'Not just for yourself. If you were rumbled it would be disastrous. I'd be out on my ear. I'm directly responsible for anyone who gets past that door.'

'All right, all right,' said Adolf testily. 'I take your point.' He was annoyed that he had been unable to put to some use the valuable lesson he felt he had learned the night of the abortive rebellion in Argyll Street. Though the young man was a minority of one, Adolf had tried to exert his authority and failed. The young man simply talked him into the ground.

'We have very little time,' worried the young man. 'The curtain will be down at any moment.'

'Rubbish,' said Adolf. 'They haven't yet finished the Pavilion Duet.' He had seen *The Merry Widow* seven times. It was his favourite operetta.

The change had to be accomplished within the constricted space of the cubby hole in the wall. There was nowhere else that was safe.

'Oh my God!' protested Adolf, when he saw the garments that were handed to him. 'Surely you can find something less conspicuous.'

'It's the safest costume in the world,' the young man assured him. 'For a man in your position.'

He should know, thought Adolf. Resigned, he stepped into the voluminous skirt and struggled to fasten the innumerable hooks and eyes of a blue voile blouse.

'Hurry,' the young man urged. 'They are coming to the end of the finale.'

Thanking his stars that he hadn't been given a bonnet, Adolf draped a grey shawl over his head and stepped down into the passage.

'Out,' said the young man, and opening the street door he pushed Adolf into the night.

He walked so rapidly and with head so inclined to the ground that he couldn't tell if people regarded him suspiciously or not. He was no longer concerned about being arrested. He had done his best. There was nothing further he could do. Indeed his anxieties were now centred on how he should proceed if he reached Stanhope Street safely. He could no longer stay in England. He was a marked man. He had three weeks' wages saved and four shillings and threepence in tips. He didn't think it would be sufficient to buy him a ticket for the steamer and the train. And he would need other clothes. He could hardly go to Lime Street Station wearing the distinctive grey uniform of the Adelphi Hotel.

He had meant when he arrived at the house to creep up the stairs and discard his women's clothing in the top room. Let Meyer and Michael Murphy and the youth with crinkly hair make what they like of it. But no sooner had he entered the dark lobby than the door of Meyer's room opened. Adolf quickly turned his back to the light and stood there, hoping whoever it was wouldn't see him. He imagined it was Mary O'Leary, attending to the coals.

He was astonished to feel two arms encircling his waist.

He struggled; the shawl slipped completely over his face. A name was breathed against his chest. His buttocks supported in two large hands, he was jiggled up and down. Outraged, he threw a wild punch and had the satisfaction of feeling bone under his fist. He was released at once. Snatching off his shawl he came face to face with Meyer.

A second figure stepped into the hall. It was the man with the beard.

32

It wasn't a commonplace misunderstanding by any means, but by now Adolf was so inured to peculiar happenings that he accepted it almost as such. Meyer acted as interpreter. The man with the beard admitted he'd been following him for weeks. He hadn't made himself known for two reasons – he wanted to be sure Adolf was who he was, or rather who he wasn't, and he didn't wish to be seen by Mary O'Leary. If he was proved wrong in his surmise he would only distress her – he had a grand little common-law wife in Blackpool. He had hoped that Adolf was his son. After all he had been husband to Mary O'Leary for one night. He was sorry to have caused Adolf so much inconvenience and regretful they weren't flesh of one flesh. This last sentiment didn't sound totally sincere; he avoided looking at Adolf's blouse and skirt.

'So he wasn't on the boat?' said Adolf.

'He wasn't,' said Meyer.

'Nor the train?'

'He's no longer a travelling man,' replied Meyer.

'It's the photograph that did it,' said Adolf, pointing to the faded daguerrotype on the mantelpiece. 'It's him, isn't it? When young.'

Meyer nodded.

'Having seen it day after day,' said Adolf, 'I believed I knew him.'

'Some people are recognisable at all times,' Meyer said, attempting a smile. 'No matter how many years later or however disguised.' The skin beneath his left eye was distinctly bruised. 'You didn't fool me for a moment. Where did you find such clothes?'

'Here and there,' said Adolf. He resolved to grow a moustache. Never again would he be mistaken for a woman. Suddenly he wanted to go home more than anything in the world, even though there was no such place. Meyer and Alois between them could pay for his ticket. He would have no compunction in asking them. Alois would be glad to see the back of him and how could Meyer refuse, having whispered Bridget's name in the hall? Never in all my life, thought Adolf, under torture or interrogation, will I mention that I have been to this accursed city, visited this lunatic island.

33

The following day, when told of these latest developments, Alois, though indignant at having yet again to fork out on Adolf's behalf, agreed that there was no help for it. Obviously if his half-brother returned to the hotel, inquiries would be made. The page-boy might remember seeing him in the corridors, the head porter and the man in the leather jacket would remember the parcel under his arm.

Wrapped in a blanket, Adolf waited while Alois smuggled the grey uniform into the hotel and retrieved his old clothes from the shoe cupboard.

'You've not exactly improved your station in life,' said Alois, handing over the shabby jacket and trousers.

'Circumstances,' replied Adolf, 'have been against me.'

South America being out of the question, Alois said he would book a ticket to Linz. Meyer suggested that Munich might be better: he had some contacts in the city

217

that could prove useful to Adolf – certain political organ-isations, certain persons of note and influence.

Certain trouble, thought Adolf, but he kept his thoughts to himself.

Four days later he left from Lime Street Station. He kissed darling Pat on the cheek and shook hands with Alois and Meyer. Despite Meyer's protests he had refused to take the black overcoat with him. In his hand he clutched the brown handkerchief Bridget had made him for Christmas.

'Say tarra to Uncle Adolf,' cried Bridget, holding up the baby's hand. The train began to move. The party on the platform waved and smiled exaggeratedly.

Leaning out of the window, Adolf shouted something ending with the words '*in Zukunft werde ich es dir zurücker-statten.*' He was looking beyond Alois at the fiddle-player.

Alois swore.

'What's wrong?' asked Bridget. 'He only said you'd get what he owed you.'

'It has a double meaning,' Alois told her angrily. 'It was a threat. He meant I'd get what was coming to me.'

'It's of no consequence,' said Meyer, taking Bridget's arm and turning her towards the barrier. 'Such a strong-willed young man. It is a pity he will never amount to anything.'